Acting Edition

Four Old Broads

by Leslie Kimbell

SAMUEL FRENCH

FOR PRODUCTION INQUIRIES

United States and Canada
info@concordtheatricals.com
1-866-979-0447

United Kingdom and Europe
licensing@concordtheatricals.co.uk
020-7054-7298

Each title is subject to availability from Concord Theatricals Corp.,
depending upon country of performance. Please be aware that *FOUR
OLD BROADS* may not be licensed by Concord Theatricals Corp. in
your territory. Professional and amateur producers should contact the
nearest Concord Theatricals Corp. office or licensing partner to verify
availability.

MUSIC AND THIRD-PARTY MATERIALS USE NOTE

Licensees are solely responsible for obtaining formal written permission from copyright owners to use copyrighted music and/or other copyrighted third-party materials (e.g. artworks, logos) in the performance of this play and are strongly cautioned to do so. If no such permission is obtained by the licensee, then the licensee must use only original music and materials that the licensee owns and controls. Licensees are solely responsible and liable for clearances of all third-party copyrighted materials, including without limitation music, and shall indemnify the copyright owners of the play(s) and their licensing agent, Concord Theatricals Corp., against any costs, expenses, losses and liabilities arising from the use of such copyrighted third-party materials by licensees. For music, please contact the appropriate music licensing authority in your territory for the rights to any incidental music.

IMPORTANT BILLING AND CREDIT REQUIREMENTS

If you have obtained performance rights to this title, please refer to your licensing agreement for important billing and credit requirements.

FOUR OLD BROADS received its world premiere at Winder Barrow Community Theatre in Winder, Georgia on March 3, 2017. It was directed by Léland Downs Karas with assistant director and stage manager Samantha Webb. The set design was by Don Wildsmith; the technical director was Pamela Veader; and the costume design was by Billie Nye-Muller. The cast was as follows:

BEATRICE SHELTON . . . . Billie Nye-Muller

EADDY MAE CLAYTON. . . . . Elinor Hasty

IMOGENE FLETCHER . . . . Linda Keller

PAT JONES . . . . Beverly Rutledge

MAUDE JENKINS . . . . Linda Moore Oulton

SAM SMITH . . . . Thomas Manley

RUBY SUE BENNETT. . . . . Nancy Lowery Powell

BINGO LADIES . . . . Karan Japps, Sharon Neal, Carol Phillpotts

I am eternally grateful to this cast and crew

FOUR OLD BROADS received its professional premiere at Center Stage Greenville in Greenville, South Carolina on September 12, 2017 under the direction of Ruth Wood, with set design by Rebekah Brock, lighting design by Taylor Jensen, and costume design by Tiffany Nave; the technical director was Thom Seymour, and the stage manager was Donna Norman. The cast was as follows:

BEATRICE SHELTON . . . . Cindy Mixon

EADDY MAE CLAYTON. . . . . Jan Anderson

IMOGENE FLETCHER . . . . Linda Forrest

PAT JONES . . . . Cindy Thompson

MAUDE JENKINS . . . . Jeane Bartlett

SAM SMITH . . . . Peter Godfrey

RUBY SUE BENNETT. . . . . .Jenni Baldwin

CHARACTERS

BEATRICE SHELTON – A former burlesque star with an attitude. Senior Citizen.

EADDY MAE CLAYTON – A former nurse and "religious" lady. Senior Citizen.

IMOGENE FLETCHER – The newest resident at Magnolia Place. Senior Citizen.

PAT JONES – A rude and pushy nurse. Forties.

MAUDE JENKINS – A funeral and soap-opera-obsessed frump. Senior Citizen.

SAM SMITH – Retired Elvis impersonator and Casanova. Senior Citizen.

RUBY SUE BENNETT – A quiet, romance-novel-loving nurse. Thirties.

SETTING

The common area of Magnolia Place –
a Senior Assisted Living Community in Petula, Georgia

TIME

Spring 1992

AUTHOR'S NOTES

If the production's director should so choose, the Bingo scene can include up to three non-speaking background actors for realism until the Bingo game ends. Then they should exit.

The residents of Magnolia Place should be portrayed as vital and real people, not caricatures in any way.

The author suggests that Pat come out for the curtain call wearing a prison uniform and handcuffs.

The characters portrayed in *Four Old Broads* are fictional creations, and any resemblance to real persons, living or dead, is purely coincidental.

Eaddy is pronounced "Eee-Dee."

Ruby Sue should never make it obvious that her romance novel is a hidden camera. This spoils the surprise.

For Nannie DeVries and Aunt Sissie Bumpus
The sassiest OLD BROADS I have ever known...

And for Momma and Daddy
I love you more than words can ever say...

ACT ONE

Scene One

(Spring 1992.)

(Opening with music and lights up.)*

(The setting is the main recreation area or common room of Magnolia Place – an upscale assisted living home in Petula, Georgia. The room is decorated in a tasteful and slightly outdated 1980s motif of country blue and mauve. A sofa and coffee table flanked by two wingback chairs sits down center. Behind the sofa is a sofa table with a silk floral arrangement. The coffee table holds magazines and a box of tissues. This is the "television" area.)

(Stage right is an open hallway arch leading to the residents' individual apartments. Up center is the double open archway leading to the medical offices and dining room. A sign with arrows indicates that the dining room is offstage right and the offices are offstage left. Down left is the breezeway to the convalescent wing of the facility, known to all the Magnolia Place residents as "the dark side.")

(On either side of the up center archway are another set of matching wingback chairs and side tables with cloisonné lamps.)

---

*A license to produce *Four Old Broads* does not include a performance license for any third-party or copyrighted music. Licensees should create an original composition or use music in the public domain. For further information, please see Music Use Note on page 3.

(Period-appropriate artwork, perhaps magnolias, hangs on each side of the archway. Downstage right of the doorway is a small game table and two small chairs. A bright poster advertising the upcoming Miss Magnolia Senior Citizen Beauty Pageant hangs on the stage right wall.)

(Downstage left of the doorway is a bookcase that holds games, puzzles, and books.)

*(**BEATRICE SHELTON** and **EADDY MAE CLAYTON**, longtime residents and best friends, are seated on the sofa. Both women have their hands full of vacation travel brochures and are planning a vacation getaway. **EADDY** has stylish gray hair. She is dressed casually in age-appropriate clothing. **BEATRICE** has bright blonde hair. She is wearing stretch pants, a flashy top, heavy makeup, large false eyelashes, and an abundance of jewelry.)*

*(**IMOGENE FLETCHER**, a recent addition to Magnolia Place, rushes in from stage right and sits in the downstage right chair. She is stylish and wears a conservative pantsuit. **IMOGENE** is pulling a portable oxygen tank and wears the attached cannula with a long hose.)*

IMOGENE. OK girls I'm back...what did I miss? Sorry...my bladder is the size of a pea.

EADDY. Well...you didn't miss much...we narrowed it down to a cruise –

*(Glares at **BEATRICE**.)*

– or a cruise.

BEATRICE. *(Excited and animated.)* Oh girls...let's go with the cruise! Eaddy...we have been talking about a cruise for weeks now...even before Imogene moved in. Oh...I would love to do a cruise... *(Dreamy.)* I've wanted to go on a cruise since I saw that episode of *The Love Boat*, guest-starring Lana Turner.

(Switch.) I guess we could go with Eaddy's *wonderful* idea and take yet *another* trip up to Helen and see that precious little German village for the umpteenth time... or well...I DON'T CARE...a night over at the Stay and Save Motor Court by the eighty-five off-ramp would work! Just get me out of this hell hole!

EADDY. *(Shaking her finger at* **BEATRICE***.)* Beatrice... language! Why do you have to be so vulgar?

(Worried.) OH...I need to pray.

Dear Lord...please forgive Beatrice for her crude tongue. I am praying for her forgiveness because I know that she won't and I do not want her to burn in the fiery pit of hell...AMEN.

BEATRICE. Well excuse me Sister Mary Holier than thou Supreme...

EADDY. Thank you Maria Von Trashy.

IMOGENE. *(Peacemaker.)* Now ladies please...no squabbling today. Let's just –

EADDY. You know I can't stand it when you act like a common heathen... RUDE!

BEATRICE. Prude!

EADDY. Witch!

BEATRICE. Bitch!

> *(Both women collapse in laughter as* **IMOGENE** *shakes her head.)*

IMOGENE. Ya know girls...I have been over to that Stay and Save Motor Court and it just reeks of the reefer since those hippies bought it. I can't even drive by there without gagging.

EADDY. I know...it's just awful. We tried to have a Senior Gals on the Go Club meeting there and Leona Bartholomew broke out in hives and fainted from the smell...right in the middle of reading the minutes... BOOM...she gagged and fell on the floor...poor thing peed on herself too –

IMOGENE. Yes...I think someone told me about that... awful...just awful.

EADDY. It really was sad. One minute she was talking about our upcoming bake sale and the next...BAM...

(She smacks her hands together.)

...she just fell right out on the –

BEATRICE. *(Irritated.)* Eaddy...I know what you're doing... stop trying to change the subject. Now I still have plenty of money that the children don't know about... *yet*...and I will pay for the whole trip...all you gals have to do is say yes and –

IMOGENE. If we go somewhere I can pay my own way...but thank you for offering.

BEATRICE. Well...I just *assumed* Frank had taken all your money by now.

EADDY. *(Worried.)* Ima...I'm not trying to get in your personal business...but...how much money did you give him this morning?

IMOGENE. *(Defensive.)* Frank is just going through a rough patch right now. He *is* trying to find a job. He said he applied over at the Burger Barn. I only gave him $200... and I told him that I could not give him any more.

EADDY. That's what you said on Tuesday.

IMOGENE. No...I mean it.

(Not convincing even to herself.) I meant it this time.

EADDY. I'm going to pray for him tonight.

BEATRICE. Ima...get serious...you have lived here for less than two weeks and Frank has come to see you at least four times to get money. Now forgive me...but this morning he looked like he had been out on a three day drunk. Does he even own a toothbrush?

EADDY. Ima honey...I am sorry to say this, but I think he looks a little like...Charles Manson... I'm just sayin'... how old is he anyway?

IMOGENE. Forty-six.

BEATRICE. Oh honey...no one is gonna hire a forty-six-year-old serial killer look-a-like to flip burgers.

EADDY. No ma'am...no how...no way...uh uh –

(**IMOGENE** *stares off blankly.*)

BEATRICE. Imogene?

IMOGENE. *(Blankly.)* The Stay and Save Motor Court reeks of the reefer since those hippies bought it. I can't even drive by without getting sick to my stomach.

> (**BEATRICE** *and* **EADDY** *become worried.* **BEATRICE** *claps her hands in* **IMOGENE**'s *face and speaks loudly.*)

BEATRICE. Oh hell Imogene...not again. Imogene...I-MO-GENE! Get it together honey...snap out of it.

> (**BEATRICE** *snaps her fingers in* **IMOGENE**'s *face.*)

EADDY. This is the third time this week...it's getting worse... check your oxygen sugar.

> *(Tapping on the oxygen tank.)*

Oh Lord Beatrice we are going to have to put a hunk of ice down her panties again –

BEATRICE. *(Exasperated.)* Dammit! OK *you* check her oxygen...and I'll get the ice.

> *(Rises to leave.)*

EADDY. *(Tapping the tank's gauge.)* No...wait Beatty... Ima honey...just take a few deep breaths. Did the hose thingy come undone from the little doodad?

> *(Both ladies begin wrestling with the oxygen tank and hose.)*

BEATRICE. No...it seems to be fine.

IMOGENE. *(In a trance.)* The reefer makes me gag...gag... gag –

BEATRICE. OK...I'll get the ice –

> (**BEATRICE** *turns to exit up center as* **PAT JONES** *enters up center. She is the villain.* **PAT** *wears a starched white dress with pockets, nurse cap, white stockings, and white nursing shoes. She carries a tray with small medicine cups and a patient list. She stops to look over her*

list. **IMOGENE** *continues her blank stare and mutters quietly.* **BEATRICE,** *seeing* **PAT,** *spins around in panic.)*

(She stops up center to look over her list. **IMOGENE** *is staring blankly and muttering quietly.* **BEATRICE,** *seeing* **PAT,** *spins around.)*

OH GOD...keep it down...we don't want *(Pointing wildly at* **PAT.***)* to hear you. Oh God Eaddy, look...she's coming over here...what are we gonna do?

EADDY. STALL!

(She begins to shake **IMOGENE.***)*

BEATRICE. *(Sweetly.)* Hello Pat...don't you just look lovely today. How are you today dear?

PAT. *(Haughty.)* What?

BEATRICE. *(Overly sweet.)* I asked how you are...um...dear.

PAT. *(Puzzled.)* Dear? Did you say...dear?

*(***IMOGENE** *rises and begins to cross center as* **PAT** *crosses down center.* **IMOGENE** *forgets her oxygen tank and her hose runs out, causing her to stop center.* **EADDY** *grabs the tank and brings it over to her.)*

IMOGENE. *(Extending hand to* **PAT.***)* Oh...hello there...I'm Imogene Fletcher –

BEATRICE. *(Covering.)* Oh ha ha crazy...uh...silly girl. She knows who you are. You and those silly jokes of yours –

EADDY. *(Nervous laughter.)* Ha ha ha –

*(***BEATRICE** *guides a bewildered* **IMOGENE** *back to the sofa.* **EADDY** *and* **BEATRICE** *look to each other for support.)*

PAT. Is something wrong here?

BEATRICE. Oh no no no... Imogene is just...we are...uh... um... *(Gets an idea.)* We are rehearsing a little skit we put together for the Senior Gals on the Go meeting next week. Imogene just *loves* to stay in her character... she's so dedicated.

PAT. *(Suspicious.)* A skit...about what?

BEATRICE. *(Grasping.)* Well...um...it's a skit about...um –

> (**IMOGENE** *rises in a trance and begins talking and flirting with someone who is not there.*)

IMOGENE. Captain Stubing...Captain Stubing...I'm so excited to be on The Pacific Princess. Could you please get Gopher to escort me to my room? And I'll see you tonight at the Captain's table...you naughty naughty boy –

EADDY. *(Quickly covering.)* It's about some ladies who go on a cruise to...um...the Bahamas on the...um...Love Boat...and uh –

> (**IMOGENE** *abruptly stops speaking and becomes angry.*)

IMOGENE. And he does not look *anything* like Charles Manson!

BEATRICE. *(Pulling* **IMOGENE** *down to the sofa.)* Um... yes...they all get on the Love Boat with...uh...Charles Manson.

PAT. Charles Manson? *(Taken aback.)* Are you talking about the psycho murderer from the sixties?

EADDY. Yes...well...it's uh –

BEATRICE. *(Quickly.)* It's a comedy –

EADDY. It's hysterical. Ha ha ha –

> (**EADDY** *and* **BEATRICE** *both begin to laugh nervously as* **IMOGENE** *looks at them, confused.*)

IMOGENE. *(Vaguely returning to reality.)* What's so funny girls...did I...did I zone again?

PAT. Zone?

> (**EADDY** *quickly covers.*)

EADDY. *(Clapping.)* ...Bravo Imogene –

BEATRICE. Oh...uh...yes...good job gal...so realistic...Oscar-worthy performance!

(Both ladies clap frantically as **IMOGENE** *hesitantly bows.)*

PAT. OK, I know something's not right here...but I do not have time for this ridiculousness... I have medicine to dole out to you old fools. If I am going to get that administrator's position...I can't stand around here all day listening to your drama.

(Looking at her list she calls a name:)

Fletcher!

(Louder:)

Imogene Fletcher!

(She recognizes **IMOGENE** *and snaps her fingers.)*

Oh yeah, you. OK here...take this.

(She gives **IMOGENE** *her medicine cup then turns and exits right.)*

BEATRICE & EADDY. *(Sweetly.)* Bye Bye!

EADDY. *(Muttering.)* God help us all if she becomes the administrator.

BEATRICE. *(Worried.)* Imogene honey...you are scaring the sh–

(Looks at **EADDY**'s *disapproving glare.)*

Uh sorry...you are scaring the crap out of us. You need to get some help.

(She takes the little medicine cup from **IMOGENE** *and looks in the cup.)*

Wait...are you sure this is your medicine? This doesn't look like your medicine.

EADDY. Hey...why *do* they bring you your medication? I mean...I'm not trying to get into your personal business...but I keep my meds in my room.

BEATRICE. Yes...me too.

IMOGENE. Really?

(Puzzled.)

Well...when I moved in...Nurse Pat came to my room and told me that she would keep it in the nurses' station...then she gathered it all up and took it with her.

BEATRICE. That's odd...that's very odd.

EADDY. Have you talked to Doctor Head about this memory thing sugar?

*(**BEATRICE** begins to laugh.)*

BEATRICE. That man is an idiot...he –

(She looks into the medicine cup.)

Honey, I really don't think this is the right medicine.

EADDY. Now...I know he is a little old and crotchety...but –

BEATRICE. His mother must have been a moron. I mean... what woman...in her right mind...with the last name Head...names their child Richard?

(Beat.)

OH and get this...his sister's name...is Anita.

EADDY. Bless their hearts.

IMOGENE. *(Takes medicine cup and peers in.)* That man is older than dirt...yes...this is my medicine...I think.

(She takes the medicine.)

EADDY. Last week...Gayle Saunders went to see him with an earache and before she knew it...he was planning to Life Flight her to Atlanta for brain surgery. She just wanted some ear drops.

BEATRICE. There's no telling what he will want to do with poor Imogene. He'll probably just wanna put her down.

EADDY. Beatrice!

IMOGENE. I don't want to talk about it anymore... I –

EADDY. We *have* to talk about that memory loss of yours miss lady. I mean...I don't want to get into your personal business...but what if it's the All Timers? I swear if you don't get some reliable medical attention you are going to end up...uh...

(She points off left and whispers:)

EADDY. On "the dark side."

(All three turn their heads in unison and stare stage left.)

IMOGENE. *(Worried.)* Oh girls...I never had these memory problems before I moved here...well...not that I'm aware of anyway. I'm taking all my meds like I'm supposed to –

BEATRICE. Well something ain't working looney tunes.

EADDY. *(Scolding.)* Beatrice!

BEATRICE. OH come on...she knows I'm joking. Don't ya crazy pants?

IMOGENE. Of course I do...ya old toothless bat.

EADDY. Imogene honey –

IMOGENE. *(Anxious.)* I'm really worried girls... I don't want to end up over on the dark side. Why does everyone call it the dark side anyway?

BEATRICE. Because...there are a bunch of pitiful old people over there sitting around in the dark...alone...drooling on themselves.

IMOGENE. *(Shivering.)* How awful.

EADDY. You know...it seems like there are more moving over there every day. I saw Minnie Roberts last week...she was fluttering about and being a social butterfly. Two days later...I saw them rolling her down the breezeway to the dark side...she was babbling like a wacko and her eyes were rolling back in her head.

BEATRICE. *(Realization.)* Yes...you're right...same thing with Joe Porter *and* Mable Dupree.

IMOGENE. *(Panicked and pacing.)* Oh my God girls...they are going to take me over there and dump me in a padded room.

(Beat.)

I'm gonna be a drooling vegetable –

EADDY. Ima honey...don't worry...we won't let that happen. Will we Beatty?

BEATRICE. Of course not sugar...we'll disguise you and put you on a bus up to Canada before that happens.

EADDY. Beatrice...get serious!

BEATRICE. *(Adamant.)* I am serious.

IMOGENE. Ohmygod –

BEATRICE. OK...good...so it's settled...if they come to take Ima off to the dark side...we will throw her in the trunk of your Lincoln and haul her off to the Greyhound station. Now...while you are at least mildly lucid Sybil... can we get back to our vacation plans?

> *(***IMOGENE** *sits.)*

EADDY. Beatrice...Imogene needs our help.

BEATRICE. And like I said...I will be happy to help her...but can we *please* finalize this trip first? Imogene may want one last happy hoorah before we put her on a bus to Nova Scotia. Now, listen...I want to plan our cruise... OK?

IMOGENE. Fine –

EADDY. OK...whatever –

BEATRICE. Now who else can we invite? We need a fourth.

> *(***EADDY** *begins to pray.* **BEATRICE** *is disgusted.* **IMOGENE** *is bewildered.)*

EADDY. Dear Lord *please* forgive this heathen woman for only caring about herself and the carnal desires of her burning loins. Please do not do anything horrible to her...such as striking her down with burning hemorrhoids. She may be a selfish sinner Lord...but she is my friend and I love her. Amen.

IMOGENE. *(Confused.)* Uh...Amen?

BEATRICE. Listen to me! I want to go on a cruise! I want to wine and dine and dance the night away.

> *(Beginning to fantasize, she rises.)*

I want to run on the beach and get my hair braided like Bo Derek. But most of all I want to meet a Silver Fox and get a little pickle tickle while I still can...without needing a nebulizer treatment afterwards.

EADDY. Beatty you really are a floozy.

IMOGENE. I can't believe you are into those one-night stands.

BEATRICE. Oh honey...I don't stand.

EADDY. Beatrice Shelton...just because you have a scandalous past *does not* mean you can't change your future.

IMOGENE. A scandalous past?

BEATRICE. Eaddy...look what you have done! Imogene was the one person besides you in this place who will speak to me like I am a human being –

IMOGENE. What are you talking about?

EADDY. Well she was going to find out sooner or later –

BEATRICE. Well it's not like I'm ashamed –

IMOGENE. *(Apprehensive.)* Ashamed...of what?

EADDY. *(Gently.)* Imogene...Beatrice here has a little secret...it's not a big deal...it's just that some people don't under–

BEATRICE. Well...it's not exactly a secret –

EADDY. Imogene it's not a big deal... Beatrice was –

IMOGENE. *(Throwing her hands up.)* Wait wait wait... I knew it... I knew it I knew it.

> *(Beat, and then, pointing at **BEATRICE**:)*

YOU'RE REALLY A MAN!... I should have known with those big ole feet of yours...and that awful wig is a dead giveaway.

BEATRICE. *(Appalled.)* WHAT?! Oh Good Lord Imogene... I am not a man... I was a stripper...and this is *MY HAIR*!

EADDY. Beatty...you were not a stripper...you were a –

> *(Grandly:)*

Lady of Burlesque.

BEATRICE. Oh hell Eaddy...I was a stripper...and I am not ashamed.

IMOGENE. *(Disappointed.)* Oh...well poo...I have to admit I'm a little disappointed...I thought it was going to be something more exciting.

EADDY. Actually Imogene...it *is* quite exciting. Our little old Beatrice here once strutted her stuff at the world-famous Minsky's Burlesque in New York City.

BEATRICE. That is until my *stuff*...strutted on off without me.

EADDY. *(With real pride.)* Our Beatrice was known as Miss Bang Bang la-Dish..."The Best Guns in the West." She could do a striptease...twirl a lasso...*and* swing both of her bullet pasties in two different directions...all at the same time.

IMOGENE. *(Sincerely.)* Well...now that's very impressive.

BEATRICE. *(Taken aback.)* Really?

IMOGENE. Sure...the most adventurous thing that ever happened to me...was this one time when I accidentally took too many aspirin and took my blouse off...and showed everyone my...uh...ninnies.

> *(Distant memory as she covers her chest as if bare.)*

Luckily...Mama's funeral was over and most of the people had already left the graveside.

BEATRICE. *(Puzzled.)* Your ninnies? Are you talking about your tits?

EADDY. Beatrice...can you please say *(Whispers.)* breasts? You are so vulgar.

BEATRICE. Tits tits tits –

EADDY. *(Not really upset.)* Stop it you old tramp.

BEATRICE. So Imogene...you don't think I'm trashy?

IMOGENE. Well sure I think you're trashy honey...but I love ya for it.

> *(**BEATRICE** and **IMOGENE** giggle.)*

EADDY. *(Praying.)* Dear Lord...please forgive these evil sinners before me...and forgive me for continuing to associate with them as I am weak and easily misled. AMEN.

BEATRICE. *(Exasperated.)* Amen! Now no more changing the subject! We need to get back to planning the cruise.

> *(Grabbing a brochure.)*

Do we want to do a seven day deluxe or –

> *(**SAM SMITH** enters from stage right. **SAM** is a former Elvis impersonator. He wears a polyester leisure suit, unbuttoned shirt, white patent loafers, several gold chains, and gold Elvis-style sunglasses)*

SAM. Hey there sexy ladies. Look who's back in town ready to shake it on down.

> *(He swivels his hips and shimmies...then grabs his back as he winces in pain.)*

BEATRICE. Oh God no.

> *(Covering her eyes.)*

Make it go away.

EADDY. I wouldn't start shaking too much Sam...since you just got a hip replacement.

BEATRICE. Sam...I thought you flew out to that Flamingo Hotel entertainers' reunion in Las Vegas.

SAM. Yeah I did...had a blast too. Everyone was there...the whole gang...Dixie, Marilyn, Jimmy and *all* the boys from the band...whew...we par-teed hard. But I decided to fly back a few days early...I got tired of all the lights and the commotion and –

BEATRICE. Couldn't get lucky huh?

> *(**SAM** scowls at **BEATRICE**...but then notices **IMOGENE**. His lustful look causes **IMOGENE** to shift uncomfortably.)*

SAM. Well hello gorgeous –

EADDY. Sam this is Imogene...she moved into Inez's old apartment while you were out of town.

SAM. *(Ignoring **EADDY**.)* Hello Imogene. I didn't think we had met. I'm sure I would have remembered a sexy dame like you. I'm Sam...single and ready to mingle.

(**SAM** *takes her hand and grandly bends down to kiss it.*)

IMOGENE. *(She averts her eyes, giggling.)* Well...hello... um...it's very nice to –

Oh well...my –

BEATRICE. Imogene...allow me to properly introduce you to Mr. Sam Smith...five-year Magnolia Place resident... retired Elvis impersonator...and the sole reason the makers of Viagra are having such a good year.

SAM. So Imogene, now that we have been *formally* introduced, would you care to escort me back to my room? We can *pop (Thrusting his pelvis.)* in some Marvin Gaye on the old eight-track and get some romance going.

BEATRICE. Why don't I just POP you in the mouth and we'll call it even?

EADDY. Sam, I think you are making our Imogene here uncomfortable. Don't you think you are coming on a little strong?

IMOGENE. *(Nervously.)* Yes...well...oh my...you don't waste any time do you?

BEATRICE. Sam has always liked to move things fast... well...as fast as he can with his pacemaker and erectile dysfunction.

(**SAM** *shoots* **BEATRICE** *a drop-dead look.*)

SAM. Well then Imogene...perhaps I could persuade you to join me tonight in the dining room for a romantic candlelit dinner? I can reserve a romantic table and bring a bottle from my private reserve.

BEATRICE. A bottle of what...Pepto?

(**BEATRICE** *and* **EADDY** *motion to* **IMOGENE** *that this is not a wise idea.*)

IMOGENE. *(Ignoring them.)* Why...thank you Sam that would be lovely... I accept. What time would you like to –

SAM. I'll swing by your room at 6:30. I'll bring the candles –

(He kisses her hand.)

SAM. And you bring the Va Va Va Voom!

(He exits with a hip swivel and shimmy, grabbing his back in pain.)

EADDY. Imogene...this is not good –

BEATRICE. That man is such a letch–

EADDY. Rumor is...he has bedded every woman in this place...well...except the two of us of course.

*(**BEATRICE** turns away, obviously guilty and embarrassed.)*

IMOGENE. Girls...I am not planning to hop in the bed with him...but a little male attention sure would be nice. I haven't kept company with a man since Bernie ran off with his physical therapist ten years ago.

BEATRICE. Wait...I thought you told us that Bernie is dead.

IMOGENE. Well he is dead to me...and if I ever see him again...he will be dead to everyone else too.

EADDY. Well Ima...there is one good thing about that memory loss of yours. If you let things go a little too far...you will likely forget about it by tomorrow.

IMOGENE. *(Irritated.)* Girls...we are just having dinner –

EADDY. Imogene honey...where Beatrice is concerned...a dinner date *IS* an invitation to the bedroom. In fact... she usually asks for a to-go box before the meal even comes.

IMOGENE. *(Sarcastic.)* There's a lot of love in this room.

BEATRICE. I'll tell ya what I would love...I'd *love* to plan our vacation. Don't make me ask again. I don't care...you old broads can stay here and knit a scarf or weave a damn basket.

(Anxious.) C'mon Eaddy...let's be adventurous again –

EADDY. *(Exasperated.)* Fine! Book the cruise...but no nude beach this time...and I mean it!

IMOGENE. Nude beach? I'm afraid to ask –

EADDY. A couple of years ago...Beatty talked me into driving down to Key West. Actually...she told me we were going shopping...and the next thing I knew we were barreling down the expressway at ninety miles an hour.

IMOGENE. So she kidnapped you?

EADDY. Yes...I didn't even have a nightgown or –

BEATRICE. Oh don't *even* start...you had a great time.

(**EADDY** *gives* **BEATRICE** *"the look."*)

EADDY. We stayed at this Bed and Breakfast right on the beach called The Sassy Dolphin.

IMOGENE. That's a cute name. It sounds fun and exciting –

EADDY. It was sassy alright...it was a gay men's *NUDE* beach resort. Everywhere I looked there was a naked man. There were pictures on the walls of naked men... even the bath soaps and breakfast waffles were shaped like a...

(*She whispers to* **IMOGENE**, *who gasps.*)

...and old Gypsy Rose Lee here –

(*Indicates* **BEATRICE** *with her thumb.*)

decided she was gonna haul her naked butt right out on the beach too.

(*Covers her eyes.*)

OH...my eyes are still burning.

IMOGENE. (*Consoling.*) Oh...from seeing all the naked men?

EADDY. NO...from having to look at Beatty's saggy behind dragging on the ground. I had to help her get her bosoms out of her armpits so she could roll over on the beach more times than I can count.

IMOGENE. Oh my –

BEATRICE. (*Whatever.*) Hey...ya only live once.

EADDY. When we were out on the beach...Beatty kept ordering banana daiquiris from this cabana boy named Juan. When she went to tip him...she would drop the money so he would have to bend over and pick it up. Well...I didn't realize what she was doing so I bent over to pick it up for her. I ended up getting wacked with her bosom in my left eye and his...*you know*...in my right.

(Horrified memory.) Well…I had two black eyes for a week.

IMOGENE. *(Laughing.)* That sounds like fun to me…well… except for the black eyes part.

BEATRICE. Well…I loved it…I went back three times.

IMOGENE. Alone?

BEATRICE. No…with my cousin Elmer.

>   *(Switch.)*

God rest his soul.

EADDY. *(Bowing her head.)* God rest his sweet soul.

BEATRICE. Lord, that man was gay as a goose. He didn't come out of the closet until he was sixty-seven. The first time we went to The Sassy Dolphin he got severe whiplash out on the beach trying to check out all those naked men. Bless his little old heart…he was seventy-two…pale as a ghost and wearing nothing but a neck brace…and a smile.

IMOGENE. *(Tenderly.)* So when did he pass on?

BEATRICE. Honey that old queen died last Halloween. He was at a costume party dressed up like Miss Kitty from *Gunsmoke*. He tripped over his feather boa in those sky-high pumps…hit his head on the corner of the coffee table and died instantly.

EADDY. It was in Elmer's will that his final wish was to be cremated…and his ashes spread across the beach at The Sassy Dolphin. He said that going there with Beatrice was the happiest time in his life.

BEATRICE. But the owner said we couldn't do it.

EADDY. Of course, Beatty took it upon herself to make it happen anyway and of course I had to go along for the ride…willingly that time.

BEATRICE. So we pulled a Thelma and Louise and snuck out there late at night.

(Fondly.) I added a little silver glitter in the urn so that Elmer would sparkle in the moonlight.

EADDY. It really was lovely…ah…precious memories –

(Enter MAUDE JENKINS. She wears a frumpy house dress, orthopedic loafers, mismatched socks, and large, thick eyeglasses. Her gray hair is a mess. She carries a large notebook overfilled with papers, fabric samples, a seamstress measuring tape, and a few silk flowers sticking out. She puts the notebook on the coffee table and anxiously begins looking on the sofa and under the cushions for the television remote.)

MAUDE. Does anyone care if I turn on *A Search for Love*?

(MAUDE finds the remote tucked under a sofa cushion. She glances at her watch and frowns.)

Oh no I'm late... I hope I didn't miss Alexia's trip to the emergency room. I have been so worried since she fainted yesterday –

BEATRICE. Don't you have a television in your room Maude?

(MAUDE glares at but otherwise ignores BEATRICE.)

IMOGENE. *(Puzzled.)* What is *A Search for Love*? Who is Alexia?

EADDY. *(Aside.)* It's a soap opera and Alexia is a soap opera character. Maude is completely obsessed.

(MAUDE ignores them and points the remote out toward the "television" and turns it on. The blue light from the television reflects off of her glasses as dramatic soap opera music* fades in and continues behind the "soap opera.")

MAUDE. *(Relieved.)* OH THANK GOD...I haven't missed much...I have been so worried about Alexia and Carlton.

---

*A license to produce *Four Old Broads* does not include a performance license for any third-party or copyrighted music. Licensees should create an original composition or use music in the public domain. For further information, please see Music Use Note on page 3.

(**BEATRICE** *quietly indicates to* **IMOGENE** *that* **MAUDE** *is a little crazy. But, as the soap opera continues,* **EADDY,** **IMOGENE,** *and* **BEATRICE** *gather around* **MAUDE,** *taken in by the drama that unfolds.*)

DRAMATIC MALE VOICE. Alexia...please don't do this...I love you.

DRAMATIC FEMALE VOICE. I'm sorry Carlton...but I can't go on like this.

DRAMATIC MALE VOICE. But...Alexia...I do love you... I know I kissed your sister...but it didn't mean anything! I swear...I love you my darling.

DRAMATIC FEMALE VOICE. Carlton...I'm leaving you...and there is nothing you can say or do to make me change my mind...and...

(*Dramatic pause with dramatic music.**)

...I'm three months pregnant!

DRAMATIC MALE VOICE. Alexia my darling...no...please no...

(*Dramatic music swells as* **IMOGENE, EADDY,** *and* **BEATRICE** *snap to attention. Each has a look of guilt.* **MAUDE** *turns off the television.*)

MAUDE. (*Slams down remote.*) I KNEW IT... I KNEW IT! I knew this was going to happen. Carlton and Alexia have been together for ten years. Now Alexia is leaving him... I just can't believe she is going to (*Grasps at her throat.*) have his baby... Oh dear Lord this is just awful –

EADDY. Maude...sweetheart...I'm not trying to get in your personal business...but...um...you do realize that none of that is real...right? Carlton and Alexia are *not* real people.

BEATRICE. Ole Alexia looks a little long in the tooth to be having a baby –

A license to produce *Four Old Broads* does not include a performance license for any third-party or copyrighted music. Licensees should create an original composition or use music in the public domain. For further information, please see Music Use Note on page 3.

MAUDE. *(Oblivious.)* How does Alexia think she can do it on her own?

BEATRICE. *(Sarcastic.)* Don't worry Maude, I'm sure everything will be alright after Alexia attempts to kill Carlton...has a nervous breakdown...recovers from multiple personality disorder and discovers that her baby was *actually* fathered by Enrique...the sexy shirtless pool boy.

IMOGENE. *(Impressed.)* OK Beatrice...*you're good*...you should write for that show.

MAUDE. Oh I know you all think I am silly with my stories... but it's all I have anymore –

EADDY. *(Taken aback.)* All you have?

MAUDE. Yes...now that Clarence is gone and the children never visit...Alexia and Carlton are all I have really... well...that and planning my funeral service.

(She picks up her funeral notebook.)

BEATRICE. *(Pissed.)* You and that damned funeral Maude. Wait...didn't you decide last week on cremation?

MAUDE. *(Indignant.)* Yes I did...

(Flipping the pages of her notebook.)

But then I decided that since the children never come see me...that I want to be embalmed and laid out so they have to look at me and feel guilty.

EADDY. *(Gently.)* Maude honey...please tell me you have given up on the idea of having everyone throw hymnals at your children to try and stone them to death.

MAUDE. *(Ignoring.)* I am thinking of "Amazing Grace" played on a harp as they lower me into the ground. I want something emotional and familiar that will produce buckets of tears. What do you think...too overdone? Be honest –

BEATRICE. Do you want me to *really* be honest Maude?

MAUDE. Of course darlin' –

BEATRICE. You *honestly* get on my last frayed nerve with this funeral crap.

EADDY. Beatrice!

> (**MAUDE** *angrily flips pages in her notebook, finds the right page, and then scratches across the page with her pencil.*)

MAUDE. Beatrice Shelton...you are no longer invited to my funeral! Eaddy you are still welcome to come...if you are alive.

EADDY. What I think Beatrice is trying to say in her extremely uncouth way...is that...*maybe* planning your trip on the Jesus bus, day in and day out is making you a little...um...distracted. Honey...when is the last time you did your hair or changed your clothes?

MAUDE. *(Sniffles.)* Well...I –

BEATRICE. Maude honey, it is depressing as hell to hear you constantly talking about cremation and tombstones. Now I am *sorry* that your kids are little assholes...but our kids are too...and we are not planning on leaping into a six-foot hole anytime soon.

EADDY. Beatrice my children are not...uh...what you just said...they are just very busy with their own lives.

BEATRICE. Well...my Meredith is certainly an ass.

IMOGENE. Yep...my Frank is *definitely* an ass.

EADDY. Maude...I am not trying to get into your personal business...but you need to get out and live honey...and stop planning on dying. Maybe you can join the Senior Gals on the Go...or maybe take a little vacation.

IMOGENE. *(Brightly.)* Yeah...I heard about this *amazing* dolphin resort down in Key West.

> (**BEATRICE** *giggles as* **EADDY** *shoots a horrified look at* **IMOGENE.**)

BEATRICE. OK look Maude...you're not crazy... I'll admit I have thought about my funeral a time or two. If I was the funeral planning type...which I am not because I am going to live forever...but if I were...I'd get cremated and have my granddaughter Fiona spread my ashes across the lawn of the Playboy mansion while my

grandson Luke plays "The Lady is a Tramp" on his
trumpet –

MAUDE. *(Sniffling and wiping her eyes.)* That sounds very
nice Beatrice.

BEATRICE. Not that I've given it much thought or anything.

EADDY. *(Unsure.)* That was...uh...lovely Beatty...thank you...
I think –

BEATRICE. You're very welcome.

EADDY. As for me...well...I have set aside enough money
for Mary and Joseph to bury me in a small and simple
graveside service.

IMOGENE. Mary and Joseph?

BEATRICE. Her children...she's Southern Baptist...don't ask.

IMOGENE. Well...I'm sure Frank will just dig a hole in the
backyard and throw me in it.

BEATRICE. Now Maude you need to put down that death-
planning notebook and do something fun. Hey...why
don't you try to get down to the dining hall before they
start Canasta?

MAUDE. *(Sniffle.)* I think I will...just as soon as my story is
over.

> *(**MAUDE** turns back to the television. **BEATRICE**
> takes the remote out of **MAUDE***'s hand.)*

Oh alright –

> *(**MAUDE** rises and begins to gather her things.)*

IMOGENE. OK...that is enough stark reality for me... I am
going to go and get ready for my dinner with Sam...
while I still know who I am.

> *(**IMOGENE** rises to exit right. An anxious
> **EADDY** quickly follows her.)*

EADDY. I'll come with you sugar and help with your...uh...
hair or something.

BEATRICE. Wait! Wait wait wait...have we made our
decision? I want to make the reservations today. Will it
be a seven-day or nine-day deluxe?

IMOGENE. Yes...sure...fine...fine...I'm up for anything really –

EADDY. OK OK...a cruise is fine with me. I guess we may as well go for nine days.

> *(Then, looking up:)*

God help me. But I still think we need a fourth.

MAUDE. *(Quickly turning back.)* Wait...did you just say cruise?

BEATRICE. Don't even think about it crazy pants.

EADDY. Well shit!

> *(**EADDY** gasps, horrified and wide-eyed – she covers her mouth.)*

Scene Two

(It is the next afternoon. **BEATRICE** *and* **EADDY** *sit in chairs on either side of the sofa with metal TV trays in front of them.* **EADDY** *is playing Bingo.* **BEATRICE** *flips through magazines in boredom. Up right,* **RUBY SUE** *has a Bingo cage set up on a rolling cart. She is spinning the balls and calling the numbers in a dull and bland tone. She wears traditional nurse scrubs. She is also reading a trashy romance paperback and is very involved in the book...at times forgetting to call the numbers.* **MAUDE** *sits on the left end of the sofa, staring at the "television" in a trance.* **IMOGENE** *sits on the right end of the sofa randomly stamping her card, but not very interested.)*

RUBY SUE. N-thirty-one N-thirty-one.

BEATRICE. I am bored as hell.

RUBY SUE. I-twenty-nine I-twenty-nine

EADDY. Beatrice why aren't you playing?

BEATRICE. *(Flipping magazine pages.)* A better question is why the *hell* am I in here with you for Bingo?

EADDY. Beatrice...do you think you could stop acting like a complete heathen? You are embarrassing Imogene.

(Looks at card and stamps it.)

OH...I-twenty-nine...I have that one!

IMOGENE. After last night...nothing will ever embarrass me again... OH I have that one too.

EADDY. Then you have never had a friend get drunk and dance on the table screaming, "Come and get me boys!"

BEATRICE. *(Defensive.)* I have told you a hundred and fifty-seven times...someone slipped something in my drink.

EADDY. *(Emphatically.)* We-were-at-a-church-picnic...ya old lush.

MAUDE. Ladies I am trying to watch my story –

BEATRICE. Maude, you look like hell...didn't we decide yesterday that you were going to get your hair done... or at least bathe?

EADDY. Beatrice...really –

> (**MAUDE** *glares at* **BEATRICE** *and then returns to watching television.*)

RUBY SUE. N-thirty-seven N-thirty-seven.

BEATRICE. Imogene...what was so embarrassing about last night?

IMOGENE. *(Elusive.)* Uh...I don't want to talk about it...in fact...let's never talk about it ever.

EADDY. *(Prying.)* What did Sam do?

BEATRICE. *(Joyful lust.)* Was it at least enjoyable? Tell me everything.

RUBY SUE. G-sixty G-sixty.

IMOGENE. *(Changing the subject.)* Oh girls let me tell you this joke I heard –

BEATRICE. *(To* **EADDY**.*)* In other words...change the damn subject –

EADDY. Imogene...please do not tell another crude joke –

IMOGENE. *(Ignoring* **EADDY**.*)* OK...so these two old ladies are eating breakfast and the one says to the other, "Hey Mabel...why do you have that suppository sticking out of your ear?"

EADDY. Imogene...please no...

> (**EADDY** *puts her head in her hands.*)

RUBY SUE. B-two B-two.

IMOGENE. *(Ignoring* **EADDY**.*)* So Mabel says, "I have? A suppository?" So then she pulls it out and stares at it for a minute and then she says, *(Laughing.)* "Ethel... I'm glad you saw this thing...now I think I know where my hearing aid is."

> (**IMOGENE** *and* **BEATRICE** *cackle as* **EADDY** *looks on, appalled. Suddenly,* **MAUDE** *turns to the ladies and speaks.*)

MAUDE. Does that mean she put a hearing aid in her butt?

(The ladies simultaneously stop laughing and look at **MAUDE**.*)*

IMOGENE. *(Sarcastic.)* I'll bet you were the valedictorian of your class.

EADDY. Beatrice...you are a terrible influence...now I have Imogene to pray for too.

(Praying.) Dear Lord...please help me as –

RUBY SUE. *(Cutting off the prayer.)* O-sixty-two O-sixty-two.

EADDY. *(Excited.)* OH I have that one.

BEATRICE. Who is that calling Bingo? I don't recognize her.

EADDY. *(Glancing up.)* Oh...that's Ruby Sue...she just started working here a couple of days ago. She is just precious. Her husband William was transferred here from Atlanta to start a new insurance agency...she has two kids...Billy Jr., twelve, and Bobby, ten. She is just as sweet as she can be...she *loves* those trashy romance novels...reads them all the time.

BEATRICE. Thank you Nancy Drew for that thorough...and in-depth investigative report.

RUBY SUE. B-one B-one.

EADDY. *(Excited.)* OH I've got that one too.

*(**MAUDE** suddenly reaches out to the "television" with angst.)*

MAUDE. Don't do it Alexia...you will regret it!

(All the ladies scowl at **MAUDE**.*)*

BEATRICE. Get a life Maude...seriously.

(Then:)

Eaddy...did I happen to mention that...Bingo sucks eggs.

EADDY. It was this...or macramé *yet* again...and the last time I took you to that...you made a noose and pretended to hang yourself.

IMOGENE. OK *that's* hysterical!

BEATRICE. Let's get out of here and do something. I need a project...something fun...and creative that doesn't involve yarn...or popsicle sticks.

RUBY SUE. G-fifty-five G-fifty-five.

EADDY. The Miss Magnolia Senior Citizen pageant is next Friday. Why don't you enter?
(*Sarcastically.*) OH wait...all the judges are women... there's no one for you to sleep with to win.

RUBY SUE. (*Overhearing.*) HA HA HA!

> (**MAUDE, BEATRICE,** *and* **EADDY** *turn to look at* **RUBY SUE.**)

Oh...sorry ladies...I couldn't help but overhear y'all... that was funny...I'm sorry...O-seventy-three O-seventy-three.

> (**RUBY SUE** *goes back to staring at her book and calling the Bingo game.*)

IMOGENE. I feel like I may regret asking this...but what is the Miss Magnolia Pageant?

EADDY. Oh...it's something one of the local ladies clubs does. Lurleen Dupree down at Belle of the Ball Evening Wear Emporium brings in a bunch of dresses and they put on a senior citizen beauty pageant...it's really sweet.

RUBY SUE. N-forty N-forty.

BEATRICE. Sweet my ass...it's pitiful...most of the contestants use walkers to get down the runway.

IMOGENE. Well isn't that just precious. Why *don't* you enter it Beatrice? Maybe you could do your old burlesque routine for the talent part –

EADDY. No...she won't enter because they won't add a swimsuit competition and let her wear her hot pink thong bikini...trust me...I've tried.

RUBY SUE. B-three B-three.

IMOGENE. Who won last year?

EADDY. I think it was Martha Parcell –

BEATRICE. No...actually it was Janette Simmons...remember?

Martha is only last year's winner by default...because Janette fell in the Jacuzzi room and broke her hip.

IMOGENE. *(Excited.)* OOO...there's a Jacuzzi here...where?

BEATRICE & EADDY. Not anymore.

MAUDE. *(Looks up from the television and scowls.)* Shhh... please girls...keep it down.

RUBY SUE. I-twenty-two I-twenty-two.

BEATRICE. All I remember was Martha's horrible dance routine. All I could do was stare at her fat butt...jiggling around in that spandex jumpsuit...ugh...she had the *camel toe* from hell.

IMOGENE. *(Puzzled.)* Camel toe?

EADDY. It really was awful. Now...was it last year that Martha's grandson flew down from New York City to help her with the contest?

BEATRICE. Yes...Steven...I think he actually brought that ridiculous leopard jumpsuit with him...in fact...I think it was his.

IMOGENE. OH? Is he a beauty pageant professional?

BEATRICE. Honey...he is a drag queen...he does a Marilyn Monroe impersonation that is to die for.

EADDY. Yeah...he goes by the name...Miss Tequila Mockingbird. He also does impressions of Barbara Streisand, Judy Garland...and Bette Midler.

BEATRICE. Liza Minnelli too...don't forget Liza...

(Then, to **IMOGENE***:)*

The gays love their Liza.

RUBY SUE. G-seventy G-seventy.

IMOGENE. So he performed here...in drag?

EADDY. Yes...it was actually very entertaining.

BEATRICE. That is probably the last fun thing that happened around here before Nurse Pat started working here.

IMOGENE. When did she start working here?

EADDY. About two months ago...give or take.

IMOGENE. Really? She acts like she owns the place

RUBY SUE. I-twenty-seven I-twenty-seven.

EADDY. Yes she does...there's something about that woman that rubs me the wrong –

RUBY SUE. G-fifty-two G–

IMOGENE. *(Glances down and stamps her card.)* OH OH...bingo...BINGO!!

EADDY. WELL CRAP ON A CRACKER!

> *(She throws down her stamper.)*

BEATRICE. *(Throws magazine down.)* Thank God...let's get outta here before they come in here and make us crochet an afghan.

> *(Rises to leave.)*

IMOGENE. So what now? Arts and Crafts or slash our wrists?

> *(**RUBY SUE** crosses down to the sofa and hands **IMOGENE** a little mini box of chocolates.)*

RUBY SUE. Hey Ms. Fletcher...I know there's not normally a prize...but I just wanted to give you a little something for winning... I hope you like chocolates.

EADDY. Well...how nice...see I told y'all...she is just as sweet as she can be.

IMOGENE. Well thank you darlin'...that is so sweet...but I really shouldn't...my sugar is not good.

BEATRICE. *(Grabbing the box.)* I'll eat 'em –

RUBY SUE. Oh don't worry...they're sugar-free –

BEATRICE. *(Tossing the box on the coffee table.)* Ugh...never mind –

RUBY SUE. Well anyway...thank you ladies for playing. I hope y'all had fun... I look forward to doing this again. I just love hearing y'all's stories and jokes...oh...for those of you who are waiting...someone will be back shortly with your afternoon medication.

> *(**RUBY SUE** exits with the Bingo cart. **MAUDE** sneaks the box of chocolate and begins eating from it.)*

BEATRICE. Alright Imogene…no more stalling. What was so awful about last night?

IMOGENE. Beatrice! Can we please not talk about it?

EADDY. Sam didn't do anything inappropriate did he?

BEATRICE. OH I hope he did. Did he at least try to touch your ninnies?

EADDY. Beatrice you are so vile.

BEATRICE. *(Defensive.)* I could have said tits!

IMOGENE. I wish that was all…girls…please just change the subject. Let's go and –

BEATRICE. *(Cutting her off.)* Now don't be embarrassed…we won't judge you…much. Just tell us every hot and juicy detail…slowly…it's been a while for me…

IMOGENE. Oh it's just awful.

EADDY. *(Patting **IMOGENE**'s hand.)* It's OK sugar…take your time.

> (**IMOGENE** *takes a moment as* **BEATRICE** *and* **EADDY** *lean in with anticipation.)*

IMOGENE. OK…well, after dinner we went back to Sam's room for a drink.

BEATRICE. I knew it.

> *(Slaps her knee.)*

Ya old bimbo –

> (**EADDY** *gasps, horrified.)*

IMOGENE. *(Defensive.)* I told Sam that I am a lady…and I was only coming in for one drink…and then I had to go.

BEATRICE. *(Consoling tone.)* Honey…don't worry if you were a ho…it's OK to get a little ding a ling every once in a while. Ya only live once.

EADDY. *(Sweetly.)* Such beautiful and inspirational words to live by…you should write greeting cards Beatrice.

IMOGENE. No…I am serious…I meant it…it was supposed to just be one drink and then home…but –

EADDY. Go on –

IMOGENE. Well...I must have had one of my...spells –

EADDY. Oh no –

BEATRICE. You didn't –

IMOGENE. Yes...one minute Sam was opening a box of wine...and the next minute...things...felt all fuzzy and strange.

EADDY. Oh Imogene –

IMOGENE. I vaguely remember hearing the song "Let's Get It On" playing in the background...and then... everything went black.

EADDY. That sounds like one of your spells alright.

IMOGENE. Well...the next thing I knew...I looked over and Sam was on the floor tangled up in my oxygen hose and his head was bleeding.

EADDY. OH MY GOD!

BEATRICE. HOLY CRAP!

IMOGENE. *(Sniffling.)* ...And his dentures were out on the rug.

EADDY. *(Rising.)* Imogene...what did you do?

IMOGENE. Well...I didn't know what to do...so I gathered up my tank and hose and ran out of there.

EADDY. *(Panicked.)* Imogene...was he conscious?

IMOGENE. I don't know...he could have been dead... I just ran outta there.

EADDY. Do you mean to tell me we have been sitting here casually playing Bingo and poor Sam could be dead on the floor of his apartment?

> *(**SAM** enters stage right wearing his bathrobe and slippers. He has a big bandage wrapped around his head. He wears a hospital ID bracelet and one arm is in a sling. He limps and is using a cane. At first only **BEATRICE** sees him.)*

BEATRICE. *(Sarcastic.)* We're not *that* lucky.

EADDY. *(Frantic.)* Beatrice what a horrible thing to... I need to pray.

> *(She turns and sees **SAM**.)*

Oh Sam thank God!

> *(**EADDY** runs to **SAM** and hugs him and then looks him over and checks his head.)*

BEATRICE. *(Humored.)* What happened to you Sam? You look like hammered shit.

> *(**IMOGENE** is relieved to see **SAM** alive, but also embarrassed. She slowly rises and begins to cross to **SAM**.)*

SAM. *(Holds out his cane.)* Stay away from me you...you... she-devil. You are lucky I didn't call the police and file attempted murder charges.

> *(**BEATRICE** and **EADDY**, both puzzled, turn to look at a confused **IMOGENE**.)*

Look lady...I don't know what your deal is...but...

> *(Suddenly dizzy.)*

OOO...I feel a little woozy.

EADDY. Here Sam...why don't you have a seat?

SAM. I do not want to be *anywhere* near her –

> *(He points at **IMOGENE** with his cane.)*

MAUDE. *(Irritated.)* Excuse me...but does this conversation really have to take place right here in this general vicinity? I am trying to concentrate on my –

BEATRICE. Shut up Maude...or I will cremate you myself. Now Sam...what are you talking about?

Go ahead Sam...go on and get it all out –

SAM. Well...as you know...I took Imogene to eat in the dining room last night. After dinner...I invited her back to my room for a night-cap. She was very adamant about one drink only and then she had to go.

IMOGENE. *(Victory.)* See...I told you girls.

EADDY. I never doubted you for a second.

BEATRICE. *(Rolling her eyes.)* Whatever Virgin Mary...go on Sam –

SAM. So...we went in and I put in some Marvin in the eight-track and opened a new box of wine to let it breathe.

BEATRICE. *(Sarcastic.)* OOO classy.

SAM. She seemed all tense and keyed up...so I thought a little wine...some music...maybe a little neck massage would...you know...relax her.

BEATRICE. Right into the sack...eh Sam?

SAM. *(Glaring at* **BEATRICE.***)* Anyway...that's when she started calling me Bernie.

EADDY, IMOGENE & BEATRICE. Bernie?

IMOGENE. *(Puzzled.)* I started calling you Bernie? Oh no... I –

SAM. Yes you did and you know you did...so don't deny it. *(To* **EADDY** *and* **BEATRICE.***)* Then she started carrying on about how I was a liar and a no good two-timing dog. *(Back to* **IMOGENE.***)* By the way...who the hell is Brenda?

IMOGENE. Brenda...uh...yeah...Brenda is the gold-digging physical therapist that my ex-husband Bernie ran off with.

SAM. Well you're obviously not too fond of her.

IMOGENE. Well...no –

EADDY. Sam...there's a little something you need to know about Imogene

SAM. I know all I ever want to know...just keep her away –

EADDY. Seriously Sam...Imogene has been having a little memory problem.

BEATRICE. Sam...please tell us what happened...Imogene doesn't remember anything except you lying out on the rug.

IMOGENE. I'm not sure I want to know.

SAM. What do you mean she doesn't remember?

EADDY. Imogene has been having a little short-term memory issue...kinda like a *(Air quotes.)* "senior moment" kind of thing...but worse.

BEATRICE. She's not certifiably crazy...she's just...uh...crazy-ish.

EADDY. We have been helping her hide it from Pat for almost two weeks. We don't want her to end up on the dark side.

IMOGENE. *(Tearful.)* I'm so sorry Sam...for whatever I did... I am so so sorry.

> *(**SAM** looks at **IMOGENE** for a moment and then has a sudden change of attitude.)*

SAM. *(Sympathetic.)* Well you poor sweet thing...no wonder you –

EADDY. Now Sam...you have got to keep this a secret...until we can figure out what to do about it.

SAM. Oh *of course...* I am just so glad it wasn't about me.

> *(**SAM** takes **IMOGENE**'s hand and kisses it.)*

I was just so confused after you bashed me in the head with your oxygen tank.

> *(**IMOGENE** is mortified as **BEATRICE** giggles.)*
>
> *(**MAUDE** rises in a huff.)*

MAUDE. Shhhh ladies...*please* keep it down... I am trying to catch the end of my story and it's getting *really* good.

> *(**MAUDE** sits on the edge of the sofa and leans in toward the "television.")*

BEATRICE. Someone please put a pillow over her face.

EADDY. Beatty!

SAM. *(To **IMOGENE**.)* Don't worry doll...your secret is safe with me.

EADDY. Thank you Sam for your understanding...

IMOGENE. Yes Sam...thank you.

SAM. No worries babe.

(He kisses her hand.)

SAM. I'll be thinking of you gorgeous.

> *(SAM kisses IMOGENE on the cheek and exits as IMOGENE giggles.)*

BEATRICE. OK that was just weird as hell –

MAUDE. What part of shhh did you not understand? I've been waiting for this all afternoon –

EADDY. Maude...I thought –

MAUDE. Shhh –

> *(Dramatic soap opera music* fades up.)*

DRAMATIC MALE VOICE. Alexia, my darling Alexia, I got here as quickly as I could. I have been so worried since you fainted at the Governor's Ball.

DRAMATIC FEMALE VOICE. The doctor thinks...oh Carlton –

DRAMATIC MALE VOICE. What my darling? Is it the baby?

DRAMATIC FEMALE VOICE. Oh...oh Carlton.

> *(Sobbing.)*

> *(EADDY, IMOGENE, and BEATRICE gather around MAUDE...taken in as the drama unfolds. BEATRICE pulls out tissues to wipe her eyes.)*

DRAMATIC MALE VOICE. You don't mean –

DRAMATIC FEMALE VOICE. Yes!

DRAMATIC MALE VOICE. No!

DRAMATIC FEMALE VOICE. Yes!

DRAMATIC MALE VOICE. No!

> *(Both VOICES weep hysterically.)*

> *(The music fades as IMOGENE, BEATRICE, and EADDY gather their composure. IMOGENE*

---

* A license to produce *Four Old Broads* does not include a performance license for any third-party or copyrighted music. Licensees should create an original composition or use music in the public domain. For further information, please see Music Use Note on page 3.

sneaks a drink from her flask. **MAUDE** *turns off the television and begins to cry, grabbing a tissue from the coffee table.)*

MAUDE. This is just terrible...just awful... I don't think I can handle this...

BEATRICE. *(Embarrassed.)* Uh...I thought we decided yesterday that –

MAUDE. *(Distraught.)* What is Alexia going to do? Oh the baby...the baby... I need to go...this is giving me anxiety.

(Rises to exit.)

I'm sorry...I'll have to get with you gals later about the cruise details... I want to talk to y'all about some new music I picked for my funeral anyway. I'm changing everything to a New Orleans theme...with a parade and a jazz band –

(On the word "cruise," both **EADDY** *and* **IMOGENE** *jerk their heads toward* **MAUDE,** *and then in sync to* **BEATRICE** *with panicked looks on their faces.* **BEATRICE** *tries to avoid their stare.)*

IMOGENE. Cruise? Did you say cruise?

EADDY. Maude...what are you talking about?

MAUDE. The cruise to –

BEATRICE. *(Stalling.)* Wait...Maude...uh...we need to talk to you about something.

MAUDE. What?

BEATRICE. Well...I...it's...uh –

EADDY. *(Gritted teeth.)* Beatrice...can Imogene and I talk to you in private for just a minute?

IMOGENE. *(No filter.)* As in right now!

BEATRICE. *(Still stalling.)* Uh...well first girls...don't you think we should...uh...tell Maude about...uh...your... uh...wonderful idea?

MAUDE. What idea?

EADDY. *(Ticked off.)* Yes Beatrice...what idea is that?

BEATRICE. *(Grasping.)* You know...the uh...thing –

MAUDE. What thing?

EADDY. Yes Beatty...what thing?

BEATRICE. *(Grasping.)* It's...uh...well...Maude...we are...that is...the three of us...uh...

> (**BEATRICE** *notices the Miss Magnolia Pageant poster on the wall and has a lightbulb moment.*)

We are...going to enter you in the Miss Magnolia Senior Citizen Pageant next Friday!

> (**MAUDE, IMOGENE,** *and* **EADDY** *all gasp at the same time.*)

EADDY & IMOGENE. WHAT?

MAUDE. *(Beaming.)* Really? Me? *(Breathless.)* In the Miss Magnolia Pageant?

> (**EADDY** *takes* **BEATRICE**'s *arm and drags her down left.* **IMOGENE** *follows.*)

EADDY. Beatrice sugar plum...I really must talk to you in private for just a teensy weensy little second.

BEATRICE. *(Pulling her arm away.)* Ow...you're hurting my arm –

> (**MAUDE** *begins to awkwardly practice her pageant walk...modeling and waving to her "audience."* **IMOGENE, BEATRICE,** *and* **EADDY** *all stare at her, horrified.* **MAUDE** *strikes a pose and exits dramatically right.*)

IMOGENE. *(Grabbing* **BEATRICE**'s *arm again.)* Why will she be getting with us about the cruise? Surely you didn't invite her...right?

BEATRICE. Well...uh –

EADDY. Oh no Beatrice...you didn't.

IMOGENE. I think I'd rather go with Charles Manson.

BEATRICE. *(Lightly defensive.)* Well...we really needed a fourth...and we were running out of options –

EADDY. *(Taking* **BEATRICE** *by the shoulders.)* Listen to me! I will *not* spend my vacation listening to that woman talk about Alexia and Carlton...and picking out songs for her funeral *(Building.)* or memorial...or wake or whatever the hell it is this week.

(Appalled with herself.)

Listen to me...I'm turning into you!

(Looking up.)

Lord...please forgive me for the vile words that I have spoken. I promise I will wash my mouth out with soap later this evening. AMEN.

IMOGENE. And y'all think *I'm* crazy?

EADDY. Why didn't you ask us first?

BEATRICE. Because I didn't want to spend one more second arguing about it...so I called and booked the cruise last night.

IMOGENE. I told you I would pay my own way –

BEATRICE. Well...it's too late...so get over it.

(Excited switch.)

The cruise line is calling it a Sassy Seniors Cruise...it sails through the Caribbean.

EADDY. I am not sailing anywhere...with Maude Jenkins.

BEATRICE. Don't get your panties in a wad...I will room with Maude. I have enough drugs I can slip her to knock her out most of the trip. So...pack your bikinis girls... because we leave in less than a week for nine glorious days of fun in the sun.

EADDY. *(Goading.)* Don't you mean nine days on your back with your legs thrown up in the air?

BEATRICE. *(Unfazed.)* Probably not *all* nine...there are a few sights I want to see.

IMOGENE. Wait...did you say...in a week?

BEATRICE. Yes...next Saturday...the day after the Miss Magnolia Pageant.

(**MAUDE** *re-enters and calls out to the ladies as she models and waves. She carries a bouquet of plastic flowers and has a small lamp shade on her head.*)

MAUDE. LOOK GIRLS...what do you think?

BEATRICE. OH MY GOD –

IMOGENE. OH NO –

EADDY. Now...not only do we have to go on a vacation with her...we have to give her a makeover and put her in a pageant.

IMOGENE. It'll be like putting lipstick on a pig –

(**BEATRICE** *crosses to* **MAUDE**, *closely followed by* **EADDY**. *They both give her the once-over.*)

(**IMOGENE** *watches but slowly enters into one of her memory-loss episodes.*)

BEATRICE. Very good Maude...but there's a few things we need to work on...like that hair and um...just...well...everything actually.

MAUDE. *(Oblivious.)* This is so exciting...oh...I think I just tinkled a little.

BEATRICE. Maybe you can do that for the talent portion.

EADDY. Beatty!

BEATRICE. Or not...what do you think Imogene?

(**IMOGENE** *is now in the middle of an "episode" as she extends her hand to* **BEATRICE**.)

IMOGENE. Oh hello...I'm Imogene. Can you tell me where I can find the closest ladies room?

BEATRICE. Oh goodie...it's time for another trip on the crazy train...

(**EADDY** *immediately needs to get* **MAUDE** *out of the way.*)

EADDY. Uh...Maude honey...why don't you run on back to your room and we will be there in just a tish to start working on your modeling.

(**EADDY** *pushes* **MAUDE** *toward the stage right door.*)

MAUDE. OH OK...I need to see if I can find my extra turbo strength girdle anyway. Oh I am so excited...what am I going to wear? I wonder if I should sing...do you think I should sing? Maybe I could do a dramatic monologue... I did theatre in high school and everyone said I was –

(**MAUDE**'s *voice trails as she exits right doing pageant waves and blowing kisses.*)

BEATRICE. (*Hurrying her.*) OK darlin'...toodle-oo.

EADDY. We'll see ya soon...bye now sweetie.

(*Abrupt change in tone as she turns to* **IMOGENE.**)

Imogene...this is too much. What are we gonna do now?

IMOGENE. (*Blankly to* **EADDY.**) Hello...it's so nice to meet you. Please excuse me...I know I must look a mess... I need to go freshen up just a bit.

(**IMOGENE** *is confused as she turns to exit, not knowing where to go.*)

BEATRICE. Go pull up the Lincoln Eaddy...I'll pack her a bag...it looks like we are about to make a run for the border.

(**EADDY** *crosses to* **IMOGENE** *and guides her back to the sofa. They sit.*)

EADDY. Imogene honey...this is the limit...now sit down and talk to us.

IMOGENE. Well...alright...but who are you?

BEATRICE. Honey...you need to get it together...this is not good... I –

(**PAT** *and* **RUBY SUE** *enter.* **PAT** *now wears a pantsuit and scarf. She carries a clipboard and wears a whistle around her neck.* **RUBY SUE** *carries the tray of "medicine." She is also* *reading her paperback romance.* **PAT** *checks her watch, looks at her list, and then blows her whistle.)*

PAT. Alright...listen up people. As of today I have been appointed the new administrator of Magnolia Place... and things are going to change around here. Doctor Head has taken a leave of absence. Now...this is...

*(Gesturing to **RUBY SUE**.)*

...um...what's your name?

*(**RUBY SUE** glances up from her romance novel, which she never puts down.)*

RUBY SUE. Ruby Sue...and I have already met most of the –

PAT. This is Ruby Lou. She will be delivering your medications from now on.

RUBY SUE. It's Ruby Sue.

PAT. What?

RUBY SUE. My name is Ruby Sue...not Ruby Lou...you never get my name right.

PAT. Right...OK whatever.

(Looking at clipboard.)

We need Imogene Fletcher...Imogene Fle–

*(She notices **IMOGENE**.)*

There you are...why can't you all just stay in one place? I have been all over this building today giving out medicine. Here *(Snaps her fingers.)* come get your pills...I don't have all day.

*(**PAT** looks at her chart and turns her back to the ladies.)*

EADDY. *(Whisper.)* Imogene honey...please snap out of this. If they catch on to your problem...they are going to send you over to the "dark side" honey...we can't let that happen –

PAT. *(Back still turned.)* What are you doing? Am I seriously standing here waiting?

BEATRICE. *(Whispering and shaking* **IMOGENE**.*)* Imogene... I-mo-gene.

EADDY. Snap out of it.

> *(She smacks* **IMOGENE** *on her cheek.)*

IMOGENE. *(Clarity.)* Beatrice? Eaddy? Oh no...did I...?

EADDY. Sweetie...you have to go get your medicine.

BEATRICE. It's OK honey...we will wait on you right here.

> (**IMOGENE** *crosses to* **PAT**, *stopping to turn back, confused.)*

(Gently.) It's OK sweetie –

EADDY. *(Sweet.)* Go on now –

PAT. What part of *we don't have all day* did you not comprehend?

RUBY SUE. I don't think you should be speaking to these ladies like –

> (**PAT** *puts her hand up to stop* **RUBY SUE** *from speaking.* **RUBY SUE** *crosses to the game table.* **IMOGENE** *follows to get her medicine.)*

BEATRICE. Holy crap...Imogene is really losing it.

EADDY. *(Very concerned.)* It seems to be getting worse every day.

BEATRICE. Yes I know...listen to this. She called me this morning at the crack of dawn. She wanted me to come over and help her put together a jigsaw puzzle of a rooster.

EADDY. A rooster?

BEATRICE. Yes...she said she had been working on putting it together all morning. So I went over to her room and found her with a big box of cornflakes spread out all over the table –

> *(She begins to laugh.)*

*(**PAT** checks her list and exits. **RUBY SUE** gently touches **IMOGENE**'s arm and then exits. **IMOGENE**, still disoriented, crosses to the sofa, holding her medicine.)*

EADDY. Don't laugh... Oh shhh here she comes –

IMOGENE. Girls...I think I need to lie down... I'm going to take my medicine in my room.

EADDY. I think I will go with you sweetie.

BEATRICE. OK c'mon let's both walk Ima back to her room and make sure she takes her meds.

> *(Takes the cup from **IMOGENE** and looks in it.)*

Wait Imogene...I thought you were taking some kind of medication for your memory and your blood pressure –

IMOGENE. I am...why?

BEATRICE. This is definitely not your medicine. In fact –

> *(She pulls a pill out, examines it, then licks it and pops it in her mouth.)*

This one is a breath mint.

IMOGENE. What?

> *(**IMOGENE** takes the cup, pulls out a pill, and holds it out for the others to see.)*

And these two are just baby aspirin.

EADDY. *(Highly irritated.)* Well this is the limit! C'mon... let's go find Pat and get your right meds.

> *(**BEATRICE** and **IMOGENE** turn to exit.)*

BEATRICE. No...wait a minute girls...something is very fishy here... I don't think this was an accident. Let me see that medicine cup again.

> *(**BEATRICE** takes the cup and looks in it. She pulls out a pill.)*

OK...mints...baby aspirin...what is this one?

> *(She licks it.)*

Ugh...no...definitely not a mint.

IMOGENE. *(Confused.)* What do you mean...fishy?

EADDY. Surely you don't think they would intentionally –

BEATRICE. That is *exactly* what I think.

IMOGENE. But why...why would someone give me the wrong medicine intentionally?

BEATRICE. I'm not one hundred percent sure...but Imogene *do not* take any more pills that Pat gives you.

EADDY. *(Shocked.)* Oh Beatty...I think I see where you're going with this.

IMOGENE. Wait...what are you talking about?

BEATRICE. C'mon girls...we've got some spying to do.

IMOGENE. Spying? Who are we spying on? What exactly is happening right now?

BEATRICE. Let's go to my room. We need some spying supplies. *(To* **EADDY**.*)* Now...I want you to take this pill to Maynard at the pharmacy tomorrow and find out exactly what it is.

EADDY. OOO this is kind of exciting...like Charlie's Angels!! OOO I want to be Farrah –

IMOGENE. What are we planning? Who are we spying on? I'm very confused.

BEATRICE. Don't worry...I'll explain everything –

> *(***PAT** *re-enters, followed by* **RUBY SUE***, who is reading her romance novel.)*

PAT. Ladies...I forgot to mention our new medication policy earlier. We will be collecting all medications and dispensing them to you from now on. Cindy Lou will be by later to collect them.

> *(***PAT** *flashes a devilish smile, turns on her heel and exits, followed by* **RUBY SUE***.)*

After you learn the rounds...I will have you do the medication for this wing.

EADDY. OH Beatty...what are we going to do? I'm scared.

BEATRICE. I don't know sweetheart...but don't worry...we will fix this...but it's gotta happen fast...let's go.

IMOGENE. Ladies...wait...wait...there's something I really need to ask you.

BEATRICE & EADDY. *(Exasperated.)* What? What Imogene?

　　　　(Pause.)

IMOGENE. What exactly *is* a camel toe?

Scene Three

(Later that same evening – midnight. The stage is dimly lit. Offstage we hear a bang and breaking glass...then we hear the ladies begin to argue.)

IMOGENE. *(Offstage.)* OUCH!

EADDY. *(Offstage.)* Sorry.

BEATRICE. *(Offstage.)* Do you think you could be a little louder? I don't think they heard us over in Valdosta.

(We see the beams of three flashlights coming from offstage. The ladies poke their heads out, then enter and cross to the sofa. They are wearing camouflage jackets and camouflage hats with plastic greenery on them. **BEATRICE** *wears sunglasses.* **IMOGENE**'s *oxygen tank has a camouflage cover.* **EADDY** *carries a small crowbar.* **BEATRICE** *carries several file folders filled with papers, a VHS tape, and a clear plastic bag full of assorted loose pills and pill bottles.* **IMOGENE** *carries an open bottle of wine.)*

EADDY. I'm sorry...it's just so ding dang dark...I can't see anything.

BEATRICE. Well we can't turn on the lights.

IMOGENE. I'm getting a headache and I feel dizzy... I think I am going to have a panic attack.

BEATRICE. Don't even think about having one of your spells missy.

IMOGENE. Like what...like I plan them?

(She takes a big swig of wine.)

EADDY. OK Betty Ford...I'm not trying to get personal...but you might want to slow down on the booze.

IMOGENE. Oh sweetie...don't worry –

(She takes a big swig.)

IMOGENE. – It's almost gone.

> (**BEATRICE** *sits center of sofa. She places the videotape and bag of medicine bottles on the coffee table and begins to sort through the files.*)

BEATRICE. OK girls...get over here and help me look through these files and things. I have a suspicion that we are going to find something very shocking in here...somewhere...I hope.

EADDY. Shouldn't we just take all this and go back to your room?

BEATRICE. *(Irritated.)* Just get over here and help me.

EADDY. *(Looking up.)* Dear Lord...please forgive me for allowing Beatrice and Imogene to drag me...against my will...into a life of common thievery and debauchery. AMEN.

BEATRICE. Eaddy...get over here right now!

> (**EADDY** *and* **IMOGENE** *sit on either side of* **BEATRICE**. **EADDY** *can't decide what to do with the crowbar, so she shoves it between the sofa cushions.*)

IMOGENE. I still don't think that someone is purposefully substituting my medicine for mints and aspirin...it just doesn't make any sense.

EADDY. *(To* IMOGENE.*)* If it had only happened once I would agree...but honey I'm pretty sure it has happened several times.

IMOGENE. I guess you're right...give me one of those.

> (*Each lady takes a file and flashlight and begins to look at the files in silence. A few seconds pass, and then* **EADDY** *suddenly looks at* **BEATRICE**.*)

EADDY. OK...what exactly are we looking for?

BEATRICE. *(Irritated.)* I don't know...look for something suspicious...look for something that will explain why half of Magnolia Place has moved to the dark side in the last few months and why poor Imogene...has CRS.

EADDY. CRS?

BEATRICE. Can't Remember Shit!

IMOGENE. I may be crazy...buy I'm not deaf.

> *(The ladies return to looking at the files in silence. Suddenly,* **BEATRICE** *leaps to her feet.)*

BEATRICE. *(Gasps.)* OH MY GOD!

EADDY & IMOGENE. What?

BEATRICE. I can't believe it!

EADDY & IMOGENE. What? What?

> *(***IMOGENE** *and* **EADDY** *try to look at the file that* **BEATRICE** *is frantically waving around.)*

BEATRICE. This is unbelievable!

EADDY. What is it?

BEATRICE. This explains so much...

EADDY. For God's sakes Beatty what?

BEATRICE. Martha Parcell has a boob job!

> *(There is a brief pause as it registers with* **EADDY** *and* **IMOGENE***.)*

EADDY. Have you just completely lost your mind? What does that have to do with *anything*?

BEATRICE. Well nothing...but it explains why she always looks so unnaturally *("Lifting her breasts" gesture.)* perky...and now I know...it's silicone titties.

IMOGENE. *(Unfazed.)* Oh that's nothing...*I* had breast implants *and* a tummy tuck. I had a few other things done too if I'm being honest. What's the big deal?

BEATRICE. *(Surprised.)* It's not a big deal but...shut up... really?

IMOGENE. Yes...after Frank was born...well...I nursed him till he was five...and by the time I was done...my boobs looked like two old fried eggs...Bernie wouldn't even look at me anymore. So I got some perky ones popped in there. Lotta good they did me...Bernie still ended up running off with that prepubescent bimbo.

BEATRICE. *(Shining her flashlight on* **IMOGENE***'s chest.)* I can't believe it... I would have never known.

> *(***BEATRICE** *reaches out and grabs* **IMOGENE***'s boob.* **IMOGENE** *smacks her hand away.)*

IMOGENE. I don't have them anymore... I had them taken out. I was tired of hauling them around...they were hard...like two big hunks of concrete.

EADDY. *(Interrupting.)* Excuse me...but what does this have to do with anything?

> *(They all quietly turn back to their files.)*

BEATRICE. *(Sorting papers.)* Hmmm...high blood pressure... low blood pressure –

IMOGENE. *(Casually reading aloud.)* – Glaucoma... diabetes...diabetes...arther-i-tis –

EADDY. *(Casually reading aloud.)* – Osteoporosis... pacemaker...gout...emphysema –

> *(From offstage we hear a loud bang and* **MAUDE** *crying out in pain.)*

MAUDE. Ouch...dammit...

> *(They all quickly turn off their flashlights.* **BEATRICE** *gestures to the other ladies to hide. They all slump over on the sofa and attempt to hide behind files and pillows.* **MAUDE** *enters, wearing a shower cap, bathrobe, white socks, and house slippers. She carries her funeral planning notebook. She turns on the lights.)*

Beatrice? Eaddy? ...Imogene? Hello? Well I could have sworn I heard their voices.

> *(***MAUDE** *turns to leave, turning off the light.* **IMOGENE** *drops her flashlight, hitting* **EADDY***.)*

EADDY. Ouch!

> *(***BEATRICE** *covers* **EADDY***'s mouth with her hand as* **MAUDE** *turns the lights back on.)*

MAUDE. Hello?

> (**MAUDE** *crosses to the sofa and finds the ladies trying very poorly to hide.*)

(Bright.) Well there you are... I knew I heard you in here. What are you doing in here?

EADDY. Praying –

IMOGENE. Midnight snack –

BEATRICE. Picking up men –

> (**MAUDE** *is oblivious at first and is only interested in delivering her "urgent" news.*)

MAUDE. Well...I am glad I found you because I have put a lot of thought into this Miss Magnolia Pageant...and I am concerned about the talent part. I can't decide if I want to sing or act or maybe tap dance... Wait...why are you all sitting here in the dark with plants on your heads?

> (**EADDY, BEATRICE,** *and* **IMOGENE** *glance at each other nervously.*)

(Suspicious.) Is this some sort of Lebanese thing?

IMOGENE. Lebanese?

> (**BEATRICE, IMOGENE,** *and* **EADDY** *look confused.*)

BEATRICE. I think she means lesbian.

MAUDE. Oh yes...lesbian –

EADDY. *(Adamant.)* No Maude...we are not lesbians.

BEATRICE. Well...actually I *was* a lesbian...briefly for two weeks in May of 1967...but that is a whole 'nother story.

MAUDE. So what's going on then?

> (**EADDY, BEATRICE,** *and* **IMOGENE** *look at each other for support.*)

IMOGENE. So?

EADDY. Maybe she can help...it could affect her eventually –

BEATRICE. Alright Maude...get over here. I am going to tell you...but you have to keep your big trap shut...and I am serious...this is literally a matter of life or death.

MAUDE. *(Panic.)* Oh God...what is it? Do I need to sit down? OH NO is it Alexia...maybe I should lie down.

> *(**MAUDE** lies dramatically across the sofa. **SAM** enters, wearing striped pajamas, arm sling, and head bandage. He uses his cane.)*

SAM. I thought I heard voices. Why are you girls up so late?

> *(**EADDY** becomes frantic and has an outburst.)*

EADDY. OHMYGOD! Doesn't anybody sleep in this place? We're gonna get caught...we're gonna get caught... and I'm gonna go to prison and have to be someone's girlfriend... I've seen those women behind bars movies...I know what happens in there.

> *(**BEATRICE** puts her hand over **EADDY**'s mouth and pulls her down on the sofa, crushing **MAUDE** against the sofa.)*

BEATRICE. For the love of God Eaddy shut up...shut the hell up! Do you want us to get caught?

IMOGENE. Have you just completely lost your mind?

> *(**MAUDE** struggles to sit up behind the other ladies.)*

MAUDE. I can't breathe...move...let me up –

> *(**EADDY**, **BEATRICE**, and **IMOGENE** shift around until there is room for all four of the ladies to sit on the sofa.)*

SAM. What is going on in here...
*(To **IMOGENE**.)* Well...hey there sexy mama...how you doin'?

IMOGENE. *(Flirtatious.)* Hi Sam...

BEATRICE. Maude...Sam...listen y'all come here and sit down. I may as well tell y'all both what's going on.

MAUDE. It's bad isn't it?

EADDY. Well...it's not good –

> *(**MAUDE** immediately becomes hysterical.)*

MAUDE. OH God...I'm dying...I'm dying aren't I? I didn't even get a chance to finish the plans for my burial at sea...listen...now y'all are gonna have to charter a boat and –

(*BEATRICE smacks* **MAUDE**.)

BEATRICE. Get a grip Maude...you're not dying. Now shut up and listen.

(**EADDY**, **IMOGENE**, *and* **BEATRICE** *begin to gather up the papers and files.*)

Sam you already know about Imogene's little problem... but Maude doesn't. So basically...Imogene has been a little off the beam and we think we know why. Earlier today, instead of giving Imogene her medication... Nurse Pat gave her a mint, two baby aspirin and this strange pill.

(**BEATRICE** *pulls a clear sandwich bag containing the pill out of her bra. Everyone leans in and looks at the pill until* **BEATRICE** *crams it back into her bra.*)

MAUDE. What is it?

BEATRICE. Don't know...but Eaddy is taking it over to Maynard at the pharmacy tomorrow. In the meantime... we got everyone's medicine we could find out of Pat's office...it's just all thrown in this bag.

(**BEATRICE** *picks up the bag of medicine from the coffee table and shows it to the group.* **RUBY SUE** *steps into the stage left doorway, unnoticed by the group. She holds her ever-present romance novel. Before the group sees her, she steps back into the shadows, barely visible.*)

EADDY. *And* we stole a bunch of files from the office and we're hunting through them for anything that might be incriminating...we're just like Charlie's Angels...and *I'm* Farrah.

SAM. Well...what exactly do you think you're gonna find?

EADDY. We don't have a clue what we're doing...or even looking for. We just wanna help our sweet Imogene.

IMOGENE. Oh...I love you girls so much...thank you.

(*The three join hands.*)

SAM. So what can I do to help?

MAUDE. Me too...I'm in –

(**BEATRICE** *opens a folder and shows it to everyone.*)

BEATRICE. Well...I sorta have a plan...but first we have to go through these files and see if we can find something incriminating...a smoking gun.

(**MAUDE** *picks up the VHS tape.*)

MAUDE. What is this tape...is it some of your evidence?

EADDY. Oh yeah...I forgot about that.

SAM. Where did y'all get all this stuff?

IMOGENE. (*Giggling.*) We pried open the filing cabinet in Pat's office with a crowbar. We did it from the back of the cabinet so it would be less conspicuous.

(**SAM** *is turned-on and leans in to* **IMOGENE**.)

SAM. God you're sexy when you break the law.

IMOGENE. Hey daddy...if I'm your Bonnie...will you be my Clyde?

SAM. Bang bang baby...bang bang.

(*They peck kiss.*)

BEATRICE. Please stop...I am getting nauseated.

(**MAUDE** *reads the VHS tape label.*)

MAUDE. Look...this tape says "office surveillance."

EADDY. Office surveillance...what office?

(**BEATRICE** *takes the tape from* **MAUDE** *and gives it to* **SAM**.)

BEATRICE. I'll bet it's Doctor Head's office...here...pop this tape in the VCR Sam and let's take a look at it.

MAUDE. Oh...the VCR in here is broken. I tried to watch my *Search for Love: 25th Anniversary* tape a couple of days ago...and the machine ate it.

BEATRICE. Well...I've got one in my room...we'll just watch it in there. Y'all grab something and make sure we don't leave any trace of ourselves behind.

EADDY. What do you think is on the tape?

BEATRICE. We'll know when we know. Imogene...get that wine bottle... OK...let's see...I've got the bag of medicine... hmm what else? Oh yeah Sam –

SAM. Yeah...what can I do for ya?

BEATRICE. I want you to go and get that box of wine...and bring it to my room...I think this is going to be an all-nighter.

SAM. You got it babe.

> *(Everyone gathers their things and exits right. EADDY is last and starts to turn off the lights, but suddenly turns and rushes back to the sofa for the crowbar between the cushions. She stops to pray.)*

EADDY. Dear Lord...I know I ask you for a lot...especially lately with all the things that have been happening. But, please look after us Lord...and don't let Pat catch us and send us off to the slammer. I don't think I would survive behind bars...even with Beatrice protecting me...AMEN.

> *(She looks around once more, turns off the lights, and exits. RUBY SUE steps out of the shadows but steps back quickly as PAT enters. PAT crosses to the light switch and turns it on.)*

PAT. *(Sinister.)* The Lord can't help you old broads now.

> *(She turns and exits up center, leaving the light on. As she exits, RUBY SUE steps out*

again from the shadow of the stage left doorway and crosses stage right to the light switch.)

RUBY SUE. We'll see about that.

*(**RUBY SUE** glances around, turns off the light, and then turns and exits stage left.)*

End of Act One

ACT TWO

Scene One

(Two days later. A bawdy bump and grind burlesque song* plays. The coffee table has been moved off to the left to make a dance floor in front of the sofa. There is a "boombox"-style cassette player on the coffee table, an open makeup case, a can of hairspray, a thigh exercise device, Maude's funeral notebook, a water pitcher, several cups, and a stack of beauty magazines. BEATRICE sits in the stage left chair. She is wearing a very colorful muumuu and head scarf. She is reading a tabloid magazine and has a cocktail close at hand. MAUDE is center, facing upstage. She has received a full Beatrice makeover. Her hair is now a vibrant red and has been teased and sprayed. She is wearing a very flashy ensemble from Beatrice's closet. She has on a lot of makeup and false eyelashes. Her eyeglasses are on a chain around her neck. She awkwardly dances, bumping and grinding, but not quite to the beat of the music. BEATRICE reads her magazine and is not really interested in MAUDE. IMOGENE sits in the stage right chair, watching MAUDE in horrified disbelief. She is using a folding

---

*A license to produce *Four Old Broads* does not include a performance license for any third-party or copyrighted music. Licensees should create an original composition or use music in the public domain. For further information, please see Music Use Note on page 3.

paper fan to frantically fan herself. **BEATRICE**, *never looking up, yells over the music.*)

BEATRICE. HIPS HIPS HIPS...NOW SHIMMY!

(**MAUDE** *awkwardly shimmies out. She is not wearing her glasses and can't see very well.*)

MAUDE. *(Whining loudly over the music.)* Beatrice please...I need a break...my back hurts and my feet are going numb.

BEATRICE. *(Loud and military-like, still never looking up.)* Forget it Jenkins...BEAUTY IS PAIN!

IMOGENE. *(Yelling over the music.)* Beatrice...I think she really needs a break...she's been at it for hours...

(Pointing.)

Look...her feet are turning purple.

(Disgusted, **BEATRICE** *turns off the tape, stopping the music.)*

BEATRICE. Fine...whatever...but quitters never win!

(**MAUDE** *collapses on the sofa. She feels for her glasses and puts them on and then gets a cup of water.*)

MAUDE. Thank you...oh thank you Beatrice

BEATRICE. *(Looking up at* **MAUDE**.*)* You are *not* wearing those in the pageant.

MAUDE. I know...I know...you've told me fifty times. I just hope I don't trip and fall off the runway.

IMOGENE. *(Fanning.)* It is *so* hot in here...I'm gonna have a heat stroke.

BEATRICE. It is *not* hot in here. I am telling you that your body is still readjusting to having the right medications back.

MAUDE. Y'all are so lucky it was in that bag of pills y'all found.

BEATRICE. Yes....Janette's and Minnie's too. I just wish we could have found everyone's. We're lucky Eaddy was a nurse and recognized what was what...since most of them were just dumped in that plastic bag

IMOGENE. Do you know that last night...when Pat came around with my meds...it was three Tic-Tacs and an aspirin...oh...and that mystery pill.

BEATRICE. Well we should know what that mystery pill is today...if Eaddy ever gets back from the pharmacy. She dropped it off yesterday...but Maynard said he didn't recognize it. He has to do a little research.

IMOGENE. I'm just glad no one has discovered our break-in... because we need more time to figure this thing out and gather evidence.

BEATRICE. Well we don't have time...we have less than twenty-four hours.

MAUDE. What about that...uh...video?

(All three women make a disgusted face.)

IMOGENE. *(Appalled.)* I've never seen anything like that.

MAUDE. *(Uneasy.)* I didn't know the human body was capable of...uh...bending like that.

(Each lady registers a different emotion as they quietly visualize the sex tape.)

(Distant.) Some things can never be unseen.

BEATRICE. I was thinking the same thing the third time I watched it.

IMOGENE. Did you see his –?

MAUDE. Yes...I did –

IMOGENE. How did she –?

MAUDE. I wouldn't even *begin* to know... I feel dirty just talking about it –

BEATRICE. Well...one thing is for certain...if she decides to give up nursing...she has a real future in the circus as a contortionist.

MAUDE. *(Brightly.)* Or a sword swallower –

IMOGENE. Why don't you just take the video straight to Doctor Head?

BEATRICE. Because I'm not one hundred percent sure he's innocent in all this...this...whatever it is that's going on...and anyway...I have no idea where he is. I haven't seen him in almost a week. Look...either way...Pat is screwed.

> *(She raises her drink in a toast and then takes a sip.)*

I just hope we can finish our little mission impossible thing tomorrow night during the pageant while Pat is distracted.

MAUDE. When is Eaddy gonna be back?

IMOGENE. *(Looks at her watch.)* She left almost three hours ago...she should be back by now.

BEATRICE. Well...Maynard down at the pharmacy has a thing for Eaddy...I'm sure he is flirting up a storm.

IMOGENE. Oh...so that's why you sent her instead of Sam.

BEATRICE. Yeah...and I had other things for Sam to do.

> *(SAM enters and crosses to IMOGENE. He is no longer wearing the sling but is still using a cane. He is using his free hand to rub his bottom.)*

SAM. *(To IMOGENE.)* Hey there sexy mama...did you miss me?

IMOGENE. You know I did daddy. *(Giggles.)*

> *(SAM leans down and gives IMOGENE a little kiss on the cheek.)*

MAUDE. Y'all two are so cute and romantic...just like Alexia and Carlton.

BEATRICE. Don't encourage them...they're nauseating. I had hoped now that Imogene is taking all the right medication...that she would come to her senses.

SAM. *(Rubbing his bottom.)* Beatrice...don't be jealous...you had your chance.

BEATRICE. *(Irritated.)* Whatever... Sam why do you keep rubbing on your butt?

SAM. Oh...sorry...it's just that last night I took out my dentures when I was getting ready for bed...and somehow I ended up sitting on them and biting myself on the ass.

IMOGENE. *(Babying him.)* Poor thing.

BEATRICE. You two are just grossing me out...so how did it go over on the dark side Sam?

SAM. Good...good...I found Janette and Minnie and gave them their medications...and I told them what's going on.

BEATRICE. Thank you Sam.

SAM. They both cried and cried...happy tears of course. It made me feel so good...oh and I told them to avoid that strange pill.

BEATRICE. And did you talk to your private detective friend...what's his name?

SAM. Walter...yeah...he still can't find any information on a Pat Jones before two years ago. He can't find a residence...or school records or anything. But he has some other connections and said he would try to call me later today.

MAUDE. Well...since Beatrice is letting me take a little break...do y'all mind if I catch a little of my story? Alexia is leaving for Puerto Rico today...and I hope Carlton can stop her in time.

BEATRICE. You need to be exercising...we are never gonna get your butt into one of Lurleen's evening dresses at the rate you're going.

MAUDE. *(Grabbing the thigh exerciser.)* Beatrice...look here...I can exercise while I watch my show. Please Beatrice...I haven't picked up my funeral notebook all day...come on...please?

IMOGENE. Please let her...or you'll never hear the end of it.

BEATRICE. Fine...turn it on...turn it on –

MAUDE. Yay!

(**MAUDE** *digs the remote out of the sofa cushion and turns on the television. She places the* *thigh exerciser between her knees and begins to use it.)*

BEATRICE. But now listen y'all...remember...we are running out of time and we may have to launch into our plan at any minute. So...for now...just try to act normal...

(She looks at **MAUDE***, who is now google-eyed watching television and pumping the thigh exerciser with glee.)*

...or at least as normal as possible.

(Dramatic soap opera music fades up. As before,* **BEATRICE***,* **IMOGENE***, and even* **SAM** *get pulled into the drama of the show.)*

DRAMATIC FEMALE VOICE. I told you Carlton, I'm leaving.

DRAMATIC MALE VOICE. Alexia, darling...after all these years...it can't end like this...you can't get on that airplane.

DRAMATIC FEMALE VOICE. It's over Carlton. It's over and I must go –

DRAMATIC MALE VOICE. Not until I say so...my beautiful darling –

(The music swells, indicating a passionate moment between the couple. Everyone watching reacts in different ways.)

DRAMATIC FEMALE VOICE. Oh...oh Carlton...I do still love you...I do –

DRAMATIC MALE VOICE. I'll never let you go –

DRAMATIC FEMALE VOICE. Oh Carlton –

DRAMATIC MALE VOICE. Oh Alexia –

(Everyone has become emotional...even **SAM***.* **BEATRICE** *snatches the remote from* **MAUDE***, turns off the television, and throws the remote to the floor.* **SAM** *turns away to wipe his eyes.)*

---

*A license to produce *Four Old Broads* does not include a performance license for any third-party or copyrighted music. Licensees should create an original composition or use music in the public domain. For further information, please see Music Use Note on page 3.

MAUDE. What did ya do that for?

BEATRICE. *(Wiping her eyes.)* I hope they both get on that damn plane and it crashes!

> *(***PAT*** *enters from stage left. She is in a foul mood. She braces herself on the doorway, breathing heavy.* **MAUDE**'s *thigh exerciser crashes to the floor.* **PAT** *is followed closely by* **RUBY SUE**, *who is still reading her romance novel.)*

MAUDE. *(Quietly.)* The rooster is in the hen house...I repeat...the rooster is in the hen house.

> *(The group launches into their pre-planned strategy.* **MAUDE** *picks up her funeral notebook and holds it in front of her face.* **SAM** *crosses to the game table and picks up a crossword puzzle book.* **BEATRICE** *begins to slide the coffee table back in place.* **IMOGENE** *stares off into space, pretending to have a memory-loss episode.)*

PAT. There you are...I thought I would never find you. If I didn't know better...I would swear you were trying to hide from me.

> *(***IMOGENE**, **BEATRICE**, *and* **MAUDE** *look at one another, confused and suspicious.)*

BEATRICE. What? We've been in here all morning –

> *(***RUBY SUE** *notices* **MAUDE** *and compliments her.)*

RUBY SUE. Ms. Jenkins...is that you?

MAUDE. Yes –

RUBY SUE. Stand up and let me look at you.

> *(***MAUDE**, *beaming, stands up and does a little modeling turn.)*

You look fantastic...I love your hair...what did you do... are you –

> *(***PAT** *is irritated and raises her voice.)*

PAT. We do not have time for this crap…now listen up! I have now collected most of the residents' medications…except yours. All residents must turn over their medications by this evening. Cindy Lou will be collecting them by –

>*(***RUBY SUE*** *lowers her book.*)*

RUBY SUE. *(Indignant.)* Cindy Lou? Really?

PAT. Uh…Bonnie Sue?

RUBY SUE. No…but you're getting warmer –

PAT. Um…uh…

RUBY SUE. It's Ruby Sue…R – U – B – Y – S – U – E…Ruby Sue…got it?

PAT. OK…yeah…anyway…medication will be collected –

>*(She notices ***SAM*** *is ignoring her.*)*

Excuse me Mr. Smith, are you listening?

>*(***SAM*** *stares at the crossword book and pretends not to hear her.*)*

>*(Raising her voice.)* Mr. Smith…MR. SMITH –

BEATRICE. *(Rising and speaking normally.)* Sam –

>*(***SAM*** *turns around.*)*

SAM. Oh sorry…I was trying to figure out this crossword. Hey…does anyone know the five-letter word for female dog? The third letter is T.

PAT. *(Fuming.)* We will also be having a meeting tomorrow for all the residents after that old lady pageant thing. We will need to account for the whereabouts of everyone in the building two nights ago…as it seems there has been a break-in.

>*(***SAM**, **IMOGENE**, **BEATRICE**, and **MAUDE*** *all get looks of concern and panic.*)*

BEATRICE. A break-in?

SAM. That is terrible news that I am hearing about right now…for the first time.

MAUDE. That is very disturbing and completely new information.

PAT. *(Knowing.)* Uh-huh...actually I think it's about time that I –

> *(Suddenly,* **IMOGENE** *rises from her chair as if in a trance. She has started "the plan.")*

IMOGENE. *(Poorly overacting.)* Who am I? Where am I? I have absolutely no recognition of anything or anyone at this time.

MAUDE. *(Realizing it's her "line," she tries to remember her part. She crosses dramatically to* **IMOGENE**.*)* Um...yes... OK...uh...OH NO...I think Imogene is having one of her memory spells...what are we going to do?

> *(***SAM** *crosses to* **IMOGENE** *and takes her hand to deliver his "line.")*

SAM. Oh no Imogene...what's wrong...are you OK?

> *(***PAT** *pulls out a walkie-talkie and begins to speak into it.)*

PAT. I need a wheelchair in the day room right away...a wheelchair to the –

> *(She sees* **RUBY SUE**.*)*

Oh...Betty Lou...I forgot you were here...please go and get a wheelchair and bring it here for Mrs. Phillips right away.

RUBY SUE. My name is –

> *(***RUBY SUE** *scowls and then exits quickly up center.)*

SAM. This is Imogene Fletcher...Fletcher...not Phillips.

> *(***IMOGENE** *winks at* **SAM**.*)*

PAT. Oh yes...well...don't worry...we will make sure that Mrs. Fletcher is attended to right away.

BEATRICE. Excuse me Pat...but you need to wipe your mouth –

> *(***BEATRICE** *wipes her mouth.)*

PAT. *(Raising her hand to her mouth.)* What...where?

BEATRICE. *(Rubbing the corner of her mouth.)* Right by the corner there...you still have just a tiny little bit of bullshit on your lips.

> *(**PAT** growls and stomps her foot as **RUBY SUE** re-enters from up center with the wheelchair... still reading her book.)*

PAT. Ah yes...thank you Peggy Lou –

SAM. *(Helping **IMOGENE** to the wheelchair.)* Here sweet lady...let me help you...be careful now and don't trip over your hose.

> *(**SAM** reaches out and squeezes **IMOGENE**'s bottom, causing her to squeal and giggle.)*

IMOGENE. *(Winking.)* Thank you kind sir...whoever you are.

PAT. Mary Lou...could you please escort Mrs....uh...Mrs. –

BEATRICE, MAUDE & SAM. Fletcher!

PAT. Yes whatever...to the east wing for an examination?

> *(**RUBY SUE** nods and rolls **IMOGENE** off left. **SAM** crosses to the doorway to watch as **IMOGENE** is rolled away. **EADDY** rushes in.)*

EADDY. What's going on...where are they taking Imogene?

PAT. I'll need the rest of your medications by *(Looks at watch.)* six this evening.

> *(**PAT** flashes an evil smile, turns sharply, and exits. Everyone surrounds **EADDY**.)*

EADDY. *(Confused panic.)* What's going on... I thought you were going to wait for me to put our plan in motion?

BEATRICE. Well...the opportunity presented itself. Pat made it clear that she is on to us and the break-in...besides... you have been gone for eight hours.

EADDY. I have not been gone that long. I have been gone for two hours and forty-five minutes. Maynard was still waiting for the paperwork to –

BEATRICE. *(Irritated.)* Well *I* have been here all morning trying to –

EADDY. *(Bold.)* Don't take that tone with me...I'm the one that had to –

> (**SAM** *turns around. He is very upset.*)

SAM. Excuse me...but could you please have your little lovers spat another time? Eaddy...what did you find out?

EADDY. Oh...well...it's gonna help us alright...just wait until you...

(*Switch.*) OH Maude...I saw Lurleen Dupree pulling up out front...I'm sure she has all the pageant dresses and stuff. All the other contestants are already out there –

MAUDE. *(Panic.)* Oh Lordy...Martha is going to get the best one! Can I run on out there real quick and find a dress Beatrice?

BEATRICE. Yes...but remember that we need you back here ASAP to make this plan of ours work...so hurry!

MAUDE. Oooo...I'm not sure I know what to pick...what if I pick something tacky?

BEATRICE. *(Irritated.)* Just get something that fits...

(*Aside.*) God willing...

(*Then.*) I promise Lurleen won't let you pick something tacky...and I have your tap dance costume almost finished.

MAUDE. Alright I'll be back as soon as I can...pray for me Eaddy...I'M GOING IN!

> (**MAUDE** *exits right.*)

EADDY. Tap dance? I thought she was doing some dramatic skit thing.

BEATRICE. Yeah...well after I spent most of last night watching her priss around saying "Fiddle Dee Dee" and gnawing on this nasty old turnip...bellowing, "I'll never go hungry again," *(She raises her fist in the air dramatically.)* and as God is *MY* witness...I wanted to kill her dead.

(*Calm.*) So she is tap dancing.

EADDY. Well...can she actually tap dance?

BEATRICE. Uh...well it's more of a clompy stompy thing... but believe it or not...she already had tap shoes in her closet.

EADDY. Well that is just *precious*... I wonder if she –

(**SAM** *becomes anxious and explodes.*)

SAM. Dammit Eaddy...what did Maynard say?

EADDY. Oh yeah...sorry...OK...so get this –

(**EADDY** *motions for everyone to gather close and pulls the papers from her purse.*)

Maynard had to do some major digging to even find out what this pill is...because it was only out on the market for a few months before the FDA recalled it.

SAM. What is it?

EADDY. It's called Zee-nex-uh-deen...and get this...it was supposed to help people with anxiety...but it was recalled because it caused people to have...are you ready? ...Short – term – memory – loss.

BEATRICE. HOLY CRAP!... No wonder poor Imogene – *(Then, pissed.)* I am gonna have to kick –

(**BEATRICE** *turns to leave, but* **SAM** *grabs her arm.*)

SAM. Hold up Rocky Balboa –

EADDY. We don't have all the proof we need yet. We still need to go through with our little plan to make sure we have concrete evidence.

BEATRICE. Sam...you *have* to keep an eye on Imogene...I'm not sure she can pull this off.

SAM. Don't worry...I went over and over it with her and just in case we can't get to her...she has a three-day supply of her medication stuffed down in her bra.

BEATRICE. She is our only inside source...this *has* to work. Does she have that little tape recorder?

SAM. Yep...that's in her bra too...I put it there myself...uh... OK...I'll check back in with y'all in a bit.

(**SAM** *exits as* **EADDY** *calls out to him.*)

EADDY. Tell her I am gonna say a little prayer for her... Oh I feel like I am gonna faint right out on the floor.

BEATRICE. Don't faint on me now. Listen...we got Imogene on the inside and we've got Maude to act as a decoy during the pageant. Sam is on phone duty in case his detective buddy calls or he has to call the police. You and I will scout the offices and the employee areas again for anything we can find...am I forgetting anything?

EADDY. I don't know...you're the brains of the operation. I'm gonna pray...so bow your head. Dear Lord...it's Eaddy again. I know I have been asking for a lot lately...but I was hoping –

(PAT enters, interrupting EADDY.)

PAT. Ladies...I am *so* sorry...but I forgot to tell you earlier. Our new policy requires all vacations be approved *at least* a month in advance by the head of administration... which is now of course...me.

(She smiles wickedly.)

We are responsible for the safety of our residents and we would be devastated if anything happened to any of you on an unapproved outing...so...I am so sorry, but we cannot allow you to leave for that cruise on Saturday... I'm sure you understand.

(PAT flashes an evil smile and exits just as MAUDE rushes in, out of breath. She carries a garment bag containing her evening gown. BEATRICE and EADDY are both stunned and silent.)

MAUDE. I thought I was going to die out there...those women are crazy. Lurleen opened the side door to her van and Martha and all the others leaped in and started tearing things off the rack...there were sequins and rhinestones flying everywhere. This dress fell on the ground and I grabbed it and ran for my life. When I looked back...Martha was trying to wrestle a red sequin dress away from Beulah Tucker and poor old Lurleen was hiding up under her van. I was so scared that I almost... Hey...what's wrong?

BEATRICE. Eaddy...if you don't mind...I think I will finish that prayer for you.

EADDY. *(Hesitant.)* Uh...sure.

BEATRICE. Dear Lord...get ready 'cause I'm pissed off... and I am going to kick some ass all over this building. AMEN!

(Then, loudly.) Put on your big girl panties girls...'cause we're going to war!

> (**BEATRICE** *storms off right.* **EADDY** *and* **MAUDE** *gasp, shocked.)*

Scene Two

(It is Friday evening and the pageant has begun. Light "pageant walk" music* plays. In the dark we hear a light smattering of applause and then the voice of **LURLEEN DUPREE** *emceeing the pageant.)*

LURLEEN. *(Voice-over.)* ...And of course any of the beautiful evening gowns the contestants are modeling tonight are available to purchase in my boutique...Lurleen Dupree's Bell of the Ball Evening Wear Emporium in beautiful downtown Petula. Now...thank you again... contestant number seven...Ethel Bumpus...thank you Ethel... Ethel... ETHEL! Let's have a nice round of applause for all seven of our lovely contestants.

(Light smattering of applause.)

And next...while our contestants change into their talent costumes...please help me welcome to the stage Henry Williams and his amazing magic tricks!

(There is a smattering of applause and then **LURLEEN** *continues, unaware her mic is still on.)*

What's amazing is that all these people are still alive. How in the hell do I let myself get roped into this crap year after year after year... I swear to God I am never gonna... What?... What's on?... OH SHIT!

(Lights up as the music fades. **SAM** *and* **IMOGENE** *enter.* **IMOGENE** *sits in a wheelchair, catatonic. She wears pajamas and a bathrobe. Her rolling oxygen tank has been replaced by a small portable tank and the bag hangs on the wheelchair.* **SAM** *is wearing his white*

---

*A license to produce *Four Old Broads* does not include a performance license for any third-party or copyrighted music. Licensees should create an original composition or use music in the public domain. For further information, please see Music Use Note on page 3.

Elvis jumpsuit costume and Elvis wig. He rolls **IMOGENE** *down center and then runs to each entrance to check that they are alone.)*

SAM. OK sugar pie...we're all clear...

*(***IMOGENE*** *pops out of her catatonic state and jumps up out of the wheelchair.)*

IMOGENE. Oh Sam...thank you sugar bear. If I had to sit out there in a fake coma for one more second...I would have just died. My rear end has just about gone numb

SAM. *(Crossing to her.)* Well then...come on over here and let me rub it for you.

IMOGENE. *(Giggling.)* Oh...you are such a bad boy.

SAM. I'll show you a bad boy.

*(***SAM*** *grabs* **IMOGENE**. *They embrace and kiss as his hands slowly creep toward her bottom.)*

IMOGENE. *(Giggling, she smacks his hand.)* Sam...I have got to keep my wits about me. Stop it...you are so naughty. You hunka hunka burnin' love –

SAM. Oh yeah...you didn't tell me what you think of my Elvis costume...sexy huh?

(He turns and does an Elvis-esque dance move.)

IMOGENE. You can love me tenderly any ole time big daddy...so when do you have to go out and perform for all your adoring fans?

SAM. *(Checking his watch.)* In just a few minutes...after Henry finishes his magic tricks...one of the nurses is going to demonstrate the proper way to clean your dentures...and then after that...I am going to perform two songs. I'm sorry...but I need to wheel you back out there in a minute so I can get ready.

IMOGENE. I'm just sorry I can't scream and cheer for you... since I have to sit around and drool on myself. How long until we have all the evidence we need? I haven't seen Beatrice or Eaddy all evening –

SAM. Me either...I haven't heard from them in a couple of hours.

IMOGENE. What about Walter?

SAM. Well...I gave him one of those medicine bottles y'all had purloined the other night from Pat's office and he got an unknown fingerprint off it. He has a friend at the police department that helps him out from time to time and he is going to run the fingerprints on some database and check for a criminal record or warrants.

IMOGENE. I wish we could just turn her in.

SAM. As soon as Beatrice gives me the thumbs up...I will make the call. It can't happen fast enough.

> (*From offstage we hear a crash and then* **MAUDE** *calling out, causing* **IMOGENE** *to jump back in the wheelchair.*)

MAUDE. (*Lost.*) Hello? I think I made a wrong turn somewhere.

> (**MAUDE** *enters, wearing her evening gown. The gown is hideous and ill-fitting. She can't see because her eyeglasses are tucked into the bodice of her dress.*)

Hello? Anyone?

SAM. Geez Maude...you scared us half to death!

MAUDE. (*Squinting.*) Sam?

> (**MAUDE** *pulls out her eyeglasses and puts them on, looking around, bewildered.*)

Oh hey y'all...I must have gotten separated from the rest of the herd... I can't see where I'm going without my glasses... I'm supposed to be in the dressing area changing into my talent costume.

IMOGENE. Yep...you're lost...but don't worry...you've got time darlin'.

> (**MAUDE** *begins to pace nervously.*)

MAUDE. I'm so nervous...I've never done anything like this. Am I doing OK... How do I look? My lips have gone dry... I'm a wreck.

> (**MAUDE** *does an awkward modeling turn.*
> **SAM** *and* **IMOGENE** *grasp for the right words
> to say.*)

IMOGENE. Oh Maude sugar...you are doing just great...and you look so...so colorful too.

SAM. Oh yeah...you really stand out from all of the other ladies.

MAUDE. OH THANK YOU...but you know...I don't think Lurleen meant to bring this dress.

IMOGENE. What makes you say that?

MAUDE. Because when I walked out in it...I heard her say, "Oh crap...I didn't mean to bring that dress."

IMOGENE. OH?

MAUDE. I guess she was afraid it would be better than all the others.

SAM. Yeah...that's it...that's definitely it.

IMOGENE. Well...lucky you...lucky lucky you.

MAUDE. Yeah OK...well I guess I better go get changed into my tap costume. Don't worry though...I'll keep my eyes and ears peeled for anything suspicious.

> (**MAUDE** *removes her glasses, strikes a 007
> pose, and exits, bumping into the door
> frame.*)

SAM. Yeah...I guess we better get you back out there too... we don't need anyone catching on to us.

IMOGENE. Alrighty then...let me get back into my comatose state.

> (*She sits in the wheelchair.*)

SAM. I'm just glad I could spend a little time with my sugar plum before she leaves to go cruising in the Caribbean tomorrow...in case she meets a gorgeous hunk and runs off to an exotic island with him.

IMOGENE. Why Sam Smith...I think you might be just a little jealous of me going on that cruise.

SAM. Uh...no...not at all.

> (*He averts his eyes.*)

IMOGENE. Why yes you are...look at you...you *are* jealous. You are so jealous you can't even look at me.

SAM. *(Unconvincing.)* I am not.

IMOGENE. Yes you are – *(Sexy voice.)* and I kinda like it.

SAM. Ya do?

IMOGENE. Sure...*I* would be jealous if you were going off on a cruise with a bunch of man-crazed old floozies.

SAM. *(Surprised.)* Ya would?

IMOGENE. Well sure...at our age ya don't meet someone you click with every day –

SAM. You think we click?

IMOGENE. *(Reassuring.)* Oh honey pie...we click...don't you worry...we click. But...if we don't get to the bottom of all this madness happening around here...no one is going to be clicking or cruising *anywhere*...anytime soon.

> *(***BEATRICE** *and* **EADDY** *rush in. They are wearing semi-formal evening attire. They are arguing.)*

BEATRICE. *(Haughty.)* Why are you always so damned judgmental?

SAM. Oh no –

EADDY. *(To the room.)* Hey y'all.
(*To* **BEATRICE**.) I am not judgmental... I was simply stating the obvious –

BEATRICE. Obvious to you maybe –

IMOGENE. Girls...what is going on?

BEATRICE. We just came through the back lobby...and we ran into Peggy Simpson and her granddaughter Tiffany...and Eaddy said that Tiffany looked like a pre-teen prostitute.

IMOGENE. Oh no –

BEATRICE. – And I *think* Peggy heard her.

EADDY. *(Indignant.)* Well excuse me for being an old-fashioned prude...but I think that one's shorts should be longer than their *(Whispers.)* hoo hoo.

SAM. Ladies...ladies please –

BEATRICE. Eaddy...I don't know how you do it –

SAM. Ladies come on now –

EADDY. How I do what?

IMOGENE. Girls please –

BEATRICE. How you walk around with that stick lodged so far up your butt!

EADDY. *(Gasps.)* RUDE!

BEATRICE. PRUDE!

EADDY. WITCH!

BEATRICE. BITCH!

> (**EADDY** *begins to pray.*)

EADDY. Dear Lord...the time has now come...for you to cast this vile and evil woman straight into the fiery pit of hell. We all knew it was only a matter of time before –

IMOGENE. OK THAT IS IT! THIS IS ABSOLUTELY RIDICULOUS! You two are letting all this Nurse Pat medicine nonsense get to you...and I *cannot* take it for one more second! I...have been sitting in this wheelchair drooling on myself for three days with a tape recorder taped to my boobs...my back hurts...my ass hurts...and I need a drink! SO GET YOUR SHIT TOGETHER BEFORE I SNAP LIKE A DAMN TWIG!

> (*Everyone is shocked by* **IMOGENE**'s *outburst and there is a moment of bewildered silence.*)

(Calmly.) Thank you.

SAM. So where have y'all been?

BEATRICE. We have been all over this place trying to dig up evidence –

SAM. Well did you find anything?

BEATRICE. Nothing concrete...we have searched high and low...but we can't find anything directly tying Pat to the missing meds...or the Zeenexodeen

EADDY. YET! We will...I have faith that we will. Have you heard from Walter?

SAM. Not yet –

BEATRICE. *(Remembering.)* Oh...oh Eaddy come here a sec.

EADDY. *(Irritated.)* What?

BEATRICE. Just lean over here –

> (**BEATRICE** *leans over and whispers to* **EADDY**, *who then turns to* **IMOGENE**.)

EADDY. *(Hesitant.)* Oh yeah...uh...Imogene...I'm not trying to get personal...but uh...how much money did you give Frank today?

IMOGENE. What? What are you talking about? I didn't give Frank any money...I haven't seen him in a week.

BEATRICE. Don't be ashamed honey...I still send Meredith $200 a month to help her out –

IMOGENE. I'm telling you...I haven't seen him and I didn't give him a dime.

BEATRICE. Well...someone did...because we saw him coming out of the side door counting a big ole wad of cash.

IMOGENE. Frank was here?

EADDY. Yes ma'am...and there were a bunch of big bills too.

SAM. Are you sure it was him?

EADDY. It is difficult to mistake Frank for anyone else... well...other than Charles Manson.

SAM. *(Turning to* **IMOGENE**.*)* Where would he get a wad of cash like that sugar?

IMOGENE. I am telling you the truth –

SAM. *(Taking* **IMOGENE**'s *hand.)* I believe you sugar pie.

IMOGENE. Thank you Sam.

EADDY. OK...If Ima didn't give it to him...then who did?

> *(There is a moment of silence, and then* **BEATRICE** *has an epiphany.)*

BEATRICE. Oh no...that's it –

EADDY, SAM & IMOGENE. What?

BEATRICE. Well...come to think of it...he *was* coming out of the door near the front offices...and *not* from where you are, on the dark side.

> (**BEATRICE** *and* **EADDY** *look at each other with concern.* **IMOGENE** *becomes upset.)*

IMOGENE. What is that look for?

BEATRICE. Ima honey...do you think that Frank might –

> (**PAT** *enters, followed closely by* **RUBY SUE**, *who is engrossed in her romance novel. As soon as they enter,* **IMOGENE** *slumps over into her chair and rolls her eyes back in her head, mouth gaping.*)

EADDY. *(Covering loudly.)* – And I think you should throw in some "Jail House Rock" too Sam –

BEATRICE. *(Catching on.)* Oh yes...definitely...always a crowd favorite.

PAT. *(Haughty.)* What are you all doing in here? The pageant is in the activities room.

> (**EADDY**, **BEATRICE**, *and* **SAM** *look at each other for an answer.*)

BEATRICE. We are just talking with our friends...you haven't come up with a new rule to prevent that...have you?

SAM. *(Casually covering.)* Well...I suppose I better get on out there...it's about time for me to go on stage... I'll just roll Imogene back out there.

> (**SAM** *attempts to roll* **IMOGENE** *out of the room but is stopped by* **PAT**.)

PAT. We will take care of her Mr. Smith...Bonnie Sue will take her back to her room.

SAM. *(Rising anger.)* I am not going to let you –

RUBY SUE. *(Assuring smile...she touches his arm.)* I will take good care of her Mr. Smith...don't worry –

> (**PAT** *holds her hand up to silence* **RUBY SUE**.)

PAT. What was that...not going to let me *what*...Mr. Smith?

SAM. Uh...well...I'm not...uh –

> (**BEATRICE** *gets* **SAM**'s *attention and begins to gesture by poking at her breast and then pointing to* **IMOGENE**, *to remind him that* **IMOGENE** *has the recorder in her bra.*)

(Confused.) I'm not going to let you...uh...poke her breasts?

PAT. What? Poke her breasts? Did you say...poke her breasts?

> (**BEATRICE** *slumps her head in her hands. Offstage we hear a light smattering of applause.*)

RUBY SUE. Mr. Smith...I think it's time for your performance... Ms. Fletcher will be fine...you don't want to keep your adoring fans wai–

PAT. What do you mean poke her breasts –

SAM. Uh...I...um –

> (**EADDY** *rescues* **SAM**.)

EADDY. No Pat...he said LET HER REST. He said he's not going to LET HER REST. She needs to be around people to get better. You may need to get your hearing checked Pat... I mean *really*...poke her breasts...how silly.

BEATRICE. *(Relieved.)* OK y'all...let's all head on out there...I want to *(Looking at* **SAM** *and pointing at her breast.)* RECORD Sam's performance...so I need to go and get my video *RECORDER* from my room.

PAT. What's going on here...why are you acting so suspicious?

SAM. Suspicious?

BEATRICE. What are you talking about?

PAT. Don't act stupid, you know exactly what I'm –

EADDY. Pat honey...I am very concerned about you...are you OK? I don't mean to get into your personal business... but...are you on medication? You need to check and make sure that you are taking the right medication... because if you're *not*...you can get all *kinds* of undesirable side effects. I am going to add you to my prayer list... Beatrice...please remind me to pray for Pat.

BEATRICE. *(Amused.)* Of course –

> (**PAT** *looks at each of them suspiciously.*)

PAT. Tootsie Lou...I need you to escort Ms. Shelton to her room to get whatever it is that she needed...and then *make sure* she gets to the pageant.

BEATRICE. I am perfectly capable of –

RUBY SUE. Of course Ms. Jones...right away.

PAT. Ms. Clayton...Mr. Smith...I need you to return to the pageant immediately...I will bring out Ms. Fletcher momentarily.

Thank you...that will be all.

BEATRICE. Pat...you are starting to get on my damn nerves and I –

SAM. Beatrice...let it go –

> (**BEATRICE** and **RUBY SUE** exit right as **SAM** and **EADDY** exit up center left. **PAT** begins to pace nervously. She crosses up center to check that **SAM** and **EADDY** are gone, then exits up center right and quickly returns with a cordless telephone. **IMOGENE** sneaks a peek and realizes that **PAT** is making a call. She fumbles around in her bra for the recorder, pulls it out, turns it on, and then puts it back in her bra. Holding her breast, she thrusts it up toward **PAT** and continues to hold it there while still pretending to be comatose.)

PAT. (Urgent.) Hello...Hello...turn down the radio...it's Pat... yes listen...they're on to me. I have to finish this tonight and get the hell out of here...yes I know that but...but... EXCUSE ME? SHUT UP AND LISTEN... I can go room to room and gather the rest of the medications on both sides of the building...and clean out the doctor's office. Everyone is at this pageant thing in the dining room...WHAT...you money grubbing little pig...I gave you a thousand dollars this morning! Frank Fletcher... do not interrupt me...who do you think you're talking to?

> (When **IMOGENE** hears Frank's name, her eyes fly open and her head pops up, almost giving herself away. When **PAT** turns to look at her she slumps over again.)

Look...we have to wrap this up tonight...the jig is up... so get over here by nine and pick me up... I'll get you another grand then...yes...and I have a plan to throw these old broads off our trail...yeah...we're gonna take one of them with us...yeah...I've got her right here...it's your mother.

> (**IMOGENE***'s eyes pop open again. She is terrified.*)

Listen to me...they will be so worried about *her*...that they won't even think about me. We can cash in the pills and make a smooth getaway to Mexico...we'll let things cool off...and then in a couple of months we'll find another place to open shop...now GET OVER HERE!

> (**PAT** *hangs up and drops the telephone on the sofa.* **IMOGENE** *slumps over as* **PAT** *turns to roll her away.* **PAT** *is startled by* **MAUDE***'s voice yelling urgently from offstage*)

MAUDE. *(Offstage.)* Beatrice! Eaddy! OH MY GOD...you're not gonna believe –

> (**MAUDE** *enters up center left. She is wearing a skirted sailor costume with Shirley Temple wig, sailor hat, and tap shoes. She carries a large, colorful swirled lollipop of glittered cardboard. She is wearing her glasses and immediately sees* **PAT** *and stops talking.*)

PAT. Not going to believe what?

> (**MAUDE** *looks from* **PAT** *to* **IMOGENE** *and back again.*)

MAUDE. Not going to believe that...uh...that...my costume fits perfectly.

> (**MAUDE** *does an awkward spin.*)

PAT. Well...you look absolutely ridiculous.

(BEATRICE enters from stage right carrying an older VHS-style video camera.)

BEATRICE. I think she looks wonderful. What are you doing in here Maude...shouldn't you be getting ready to do your talent performance?

MAUDE. Well I uh...just wanted to –

BEATRICE. No...don't even ask...you can't wear your glasses.

MAUDE. Oh no...I know that...I just...um –

BEATRICE. What Maude? WHAT?

(There is a tense pause as MAUDE wrings her hands and shifts her eyes.)

PAT. Oh spit it out for God's sakes –

(There is an uneasy silence and then MAUDE takes a deep breath and rapidly spills her news.)

MAUDE. I wasn't wearing my glasses and I accidentally stumbled into the old Jacuzzi room and found Doctor Head tied up and gagged and he told me that Pat is stealing all the medication from everyone and selling it on the black market.

(She exhales and takes another deep breath to continue.)

Doctor Head said that Pat tried to blackmail him into joining her with that sex tape but when he wouldn't she drugged him and tied him up.

(She exhales and collapses against the door frame.)

(IMOGENE's eyes fly open and she leaps out of the wheelchair.)

BEATRICE & IMOGENE. WHAT?

PAT. What the hell?

(PAT looks at IMOGENE with confusion and horror.)

PAT. Wait...how...how are you standing up?

BEATRICE. Well...the cat's out of the bag now –

IMOGENE. I've been faking...we found my medication when we broke into your office and I have been taking it for three days –

MAUDE. OOO girl...you are busted –

> (**IMOGENE** *digs in her bra and pulls out the tape recorder.*)

IMOGENE. *AND*...I got your whole telephone call with my soon to be *ex*-son, on tape...and it's better than a confession.

MAUDE. Oh yeah...you're busted.

BEATRICE. Shut up Maude!

> (**PAT** *takes a few steps left and then stops.*)

We've got your number lady –

MAUDE. AND YOU ARE SOOOOO BUSTED!

PAT. *(Snarky.)* What are you old broads gonna do...wrestle me to the ground?

> (**PAT** *makes a move as if she is going to run just as* **RUBY SUE** *enters down right.* **RUBY SUE** *carries a pistol and wears an FBI badge on a chain around her neck.*)

RUBY SUE. That won't be necessary Gertrude...I can just shoot you... FREEZE...FBI!

BEATRICE. Holy Crap!

MAUDE. What? Gertrude?

PAT. You have *got* to be kidding me –

RUBY SUE. Gertrude Douchey *[Do-Shee]*...you are under arrest for –

IMOGENE. Don't shoot!

> (*Completely caught off guard,* **IMOGENE** *throws her hands up as if to surrender, dropping the tape recorder on the ground.*)

Don't shoot!

(Everyone is briefly stunned and frozen. Suddenly, PAT grabs the tape recorder from the floor and makes a run for it, exiting left.)

RUBY SUE. Call nine-one-one!

(RUBY SUE chases after PAT.)

IMOGENE. Wait...was Ruby Sue wearing a badge...did she say FBI?

MAUDE. *(Stunned.)* Yes...I think so –

BEATRICE. I'll be back...call nine-one-one!

IMOGENE. WAIT! Beatrice...don't –

(BEATRICE turns and exits right. IMOGENE reaches for the phone on the sofa as MAUDE turns and runs to the up center doorway.)

MAUDE. Should I go for backup?

IMOGENE. No...are you crazy? Don't leave me alone!

(MAUDE calls out for EADDY and SAM.)

MAUDE. Eaddy...Sam...help...we're under attack!

(IMOGENE begins to dial the phone, but suddenly PAT re-enters, followed by RUBY SUE, who has her gun drawn. PAT runs up center but is blocked by MAUDE. PAT tries to dodge her but MAUDE hits her in the head with the lollipop, knocking PAT to the floor behind the sofa and out of view. MAUDE begins to "kick" and "stomp" PAT and continues to hit her with the lollipop as PAT screams for help. RUBY SUE keeps her gun pointed at PAT. IMOGENE throws the telephone on the sofa, removes her cannula, and begins to twirl the oxygen hose over her head like a lasso.)

IMOGENE. I've got your back Maude...kick her butt –

PAT. Get off of me –

(PAT attempts to pull herself up on the sofa, but MAUDE whacks her again, knocking her to the floor. MAUDE yells at her.)

MAUDE. And *THAT*...was for Imogene!

PAT. Ahhh...STOP!...Help...someone help me please –

> (**BEATRICE** *runs in from stage right still carrying her video camera and a pair of furry handcuffs. Simultaneously,* **EADDY** *and* **SAM** *appear up center.* **RUBY SUE** *remains stage left with the gun pointed at* **PAT**.)

BEATRICE. Here Maude...use these –

> (*She gives* **MAUDE** *the handcuffs and then turns on the video camera and begins filming.*)

EADDY. What's going on?

SAM. Let me take a crack at her –

> (**SAM** *does an Elvis-style karate move.* **PAT** *emerges and attempts to stand as* **IMOGENE** *attempts to lasso her with the oxygen hose.*)

PAT. Stop it...stop it...I give up...I SURRENDER...

> (**PAT** *stands up.* **MAUDE** *handcuffs her.* **RUBY SUE** *steps in to take control of* **PAT**.)

EADDY. *(Hesitant.)* Um...Ruby Sue...why do you have a gun?

SAM. What? A gun??...

> (*Seeing the gun for the first time,* **SAM** *throws his hands up too.*)

RUBY SUE. Please...put your hands down...my name is not Ruby Sue...my name is Debra Parker...Special Agent Debra Parker of the FBI. I have been tracking Gertrude for almost six months now...but her luck has finally run out.

EADDY. The FBI?

SAM. Gertrude...who's Gertrude?

RUBY SUE. Pat's real name is Gertrude Doo-shee. We think she's been running this drug theft scam at retirement homes across the country...she steals the medications and switches it out with recalled pills...aspirin...and mints. But, she made a big mistake when she messed with my father at his retirement home up in Maryland...

he's a retired FBI Special Agent and *he* caught on to her scam very quickly. He called me in to help build a case...but she disappeared.

SAM. Uh oh –

IMOGENE. Oh my God –

(**EADDY** *gushes with excitement.*)

EADDY. OH MY GOSH...this really *IS* like Charlie's Angels... AND I'M FARRAH!

RUBY SUE. She got away from me last time and might have gotten away again if it weren't for you ladies. With the evidence you ladies gathered, *my* undercover video and the testimonies of Doctor Head and Frank Fletcher... she will be going away for a long long time.

PAT. Undercover video?

BEATRICE. How did you get the undercover video...where are the cameras?

(*She looks around for hidden cameras.*)

RUBY SUE. Ha...good question. The book I've been carrying around was actually a state-of-the-art surveillance camera...the lens was hidden in the spine...we got *everything* on video.

MAUDE. Wow!

PAT. DAMMIT!

IMOGENE. Wait...excuse me...did you say Frank *Fletcher*?

RUBY SUE. Yes.

SAM. Imogene's son Frank?

EADDY. The Charles Manson look-a-like?

RUBY SUE. Yes...we approached him to be an undercover informant...he's been working for us for two weeks now.

PAT. DAMMIT! You just can't trust *anyone* these days.

IMOGENE. *My* Frank is an FBI informant?... I can't believe it.

BEATRICE. Neither can I...are you sure we're talking about the same Frank?

RUBY SUE. You should be very proud Ms. Fletcher. Frank was instrumental in us making this arrest. Now...please excuse me...I need to get this criminal booked.
(To **PAT**.*)* Gertrude Doo-shee you are under –

PAT. It's pronounced Doo-shay.

BEATRICE. Oh...I think Douchey is the perfect name for you.

RUBY SUE. Anyway Doo-shee...you have the right to remain silent...anything you say can and will be used against you in a court of law –

(Her voice trails off as she leads **PAT** *off right.)*

PAT. Damn you old broads...damn you all to hell!

(Everyone watches as **PAT** *is led away.)*

IMOGENE. *(Disbelief.)* Did that just happen? Somebody pinch me...please.

*(***SAM** *pinches* **IMOGENE** *on the bottom, causing her to giggle. They embrace and kiss.)*

BEATRICE. Get a room!

EADDY. *(Smiling.)* OH...leave them alone...I think they're cute.

BEATRICE. *YOU* think they're cute? Are you OK? Don't you need to pray or something?

EADDY. I don't know...I just feel energized I guess. I just want to...I just want to jump up and dance.

MAUDE. DANCE! OH NO! THE PAGEANT! I've gotta get out there and do my talent performance...y'all c'mon and cheer for me...please –

*(***MAUDE** *grabs her lollipop, clomps up to the center archway, takes off her eyeglasses, and then awkwardly "shuffles off to Buffalo," bumping into the door frame as she exits.)*

(Giggling.) OW!

BEATRICE. *(Pity.)* God help us all.

IMOGENE. OK sugar britches...let's get out there and watch this trainwreck.

BEATRICE. *(Adamant.)* You don't have time Imogene...you have to pack your bags for the cruise...we're leaving for Jacksonville at six a.m....and not a second after!

IMOGENE. The cruise?

(**SAM** *is crestfallen.* **IMOGENE** *consoles him.*)

Well...I guess I didn't think we would be going now with all this undercover investigation crap.

BEATRICE. That is exactly why we need to go...we need a vacation after all this drama...and besides...do you know how much I *paid* for this cruise?

SAM. *(Taking* **IMOGENE***'s hand.)* Its OK baby doll...I'll be here when you get back...come on and I will help you pack.

(**IMOGENE** *puts her arm around* **SAM** *and looks into his eyes.*)

IMOGENE. If we hurry...we might have time for a little something else too daddy –

SAM. *(Eager.)* Well let's go then.

(**SAM** *and* **IMOGENE** *cross right.* **IMOGENE** *winks as she exits.*)

IMOGENE. Don't wait up y'all –

(**EADDY** *smiles and then suddenly remembers something.*)

EADDY. OH Lord have mercy...I never went and gassed up the Lincoln.

BEATRICE. *(Irritated.)* Well get on it...by this time tomorrow I had better be on the Lido deck sipping a Mai Tai... and getting a foot massage by a very muscular hunk... or there will be hell to pay.

EADDY. You are so bossy. I can't believe –

BEATRICE. Get over it Eaddy!

(**EADDY** *smiles at* **BEATRICE** *and takes her hand.*)

EADDY. Rude.

BEATRICE. Prude.

EADDY. Witch.

BEATRICE. Bitch.

EADDY. I love you sweet friend –

> *(They both giggle and embrace in a rare tender moment...then a sudden change.)*

BEATRICE. *(Shoving* **EADDY** *away.)* OK! That's enough of that crap...you need to go pack for the cruise... I've been packed for a week

EADDY. But...I –

BEATRICE. No buts lady...go throw some panties and a toothbrush in a bag...we are leaving at the crack of dawn –

EADDY. But I want to go watch Maude's talent performance.

BEATRICE. I'll go watch the trainwreck and fill you in later... now go...GO!

> *(***BEATRICE*** *pushes* **EADDY** *off right and then exits up center as her voice trails...)*

OK Maude...don't forget...WORK THOSE HIPS...and FIVE – SIX – SEVEN – EIGHT – SHIMMY!!

Scene Three

(It is the next morning. **RUBY SUE** *enters. She is wearing a simple black pantsuit with her badge around her neck. She is talking on the cordless telephone.)*

RUBY SUE. Yes sir...of course I will...just as soon as I get Gertrude's transfer to Atlanta scheduled with the local police department...no sir...she lawyered up...but don't you worry daddy...with all the evidence we have now... she doesn't stand a chance of making bail...yes sir...I love you too. Bye Bye.

> *(***RUBY SUE*** *exits right as* **MAUDE** *enters left.* **MAUDE** *wears a tropical travel dress, rhinestone tiara, and a pageant sash that reads "Miss Magnolia." She is singing.)*

MAUDE.

HERE SHE IS MISS MAGNOLIA SENIOR CITIZEN, LOOK AT ME...DON'T I LOOK FINE?

> *(Her singing swells.)*

HERE I AM MISS MAGNO–

> *(***MAUDE*** *suddenly becomes aware that she is alone.)*

Well crap...can't a beauty queen get a little attention around here?

> *(***IMOGENE*** *enters wearing a breezy tropical outfit. She carries a small vanity case. She does not have her oxygen tank. She is followed by* **SAM**, *who is loaded down with luggage; some carried and some rolling.* **SAM** *is dressed casually in shorts, a Hawaiian shirt, tennis shoes, and dark socks.* **SAM** *strains under the weight of the luggage, then drops it all to the floor.)*

IMOGENE. *(To* **MAUDE.***)* There you are...where have you been? Sam is loading up the last of the luggage and then we are taking off for Florida...the ship sails at 5:30 this afternoon.

MAUDE. I went over to see Janette and Minnie on the dark side...the new nurses and doctor the FBI sent in last night are still sorting out the medications...why are we leaving so early anyway?

IMOGENE. Beatrice wants to get there and board early so she can stake her claim on *all* the eligible men.

MAUDE. *(Gloating.)* Well, with my gorgeous makeover and new title as Miss Magnolia...I may just give Beatrice a run for her money –

SAM. Maude darlin'...you might want to give Beatrice her space...or *you* might end up floating in the ocean on a life raft.

> *(***BEATRICE*** and* **EADDY** *enter.* **BEATRICE** *wears a Hawaiian muumuu, colorful lei, and big sunglasses. She carries three brightly colored floral leis.* **EADDY** *wears a colorful sundress and straw hat. She carries a straw beach bag and book.)*

BEATRICE. Hey girls...who wants to get laid?

> *(***BEATRICE** *places a lei around each of their necks.)*

EADDY. Seriously Beatty...isn't it just a bit too early for this...can't you at least wait until we get to the ship –

BEATRICE. Listen Grandma...you are not going to ruin my good time this –

EADDY. Are you serious? Beatrice...you are going to have nine whole days to behave like a heathen...can you just be normal for one day please?

BEATRICE. Sugar...I tried being normal once and it was the worst fifteen minutes of my entire life.

EADDY. There is no help for you!

MAUDE. Girls...please stop squabbling...you are ruining my Miss Magnolia win afterglow.

BEATRICE. I still can't believe you won.
(To the others.) Can you believe she won?

MAUDE. *(Gloating.)* Everyone can't be Queen, Beatrice... someone has to clap when I walk by.

EADDY. Don't be jealous Beatrice...you can always enter next year.

BEATRICE. Hell will sooner freeze over... OK y'all...does everyone have everything they need? I'm ready to hit the road...Sam...get those bags in the car...let's go let's go...move it, move it –

SAM. Ma'am...yes ma'am!

> *(***SAM*** salutes ***BEATRICE*** and begins to gather up the luggage. He gathers up a few pieces and exits right.)*

IMOGENE. Hey girls...I need to tell you something...I hope you don't mind but –

> *(***RUBY SUE*** enters, interrupting ***IMOGENE***.)*

RUBY SUE. Well ladies...it looks like you are off to have a good time.

BEATRICE. We will if we ever get there.

RUBY SUE. What all do you have planned?

EADDY. Well...I brought a good book...I thought I would spend some time in the sun reading.

MAUDE. I want to go to the spa...and get a massage and one of those body scrub thingies.

BEATRICE. If you need me...I'll be in one of the bars...I'll be the one dancing on top of it.

EADDY. Shocker.

RUBY SUE. What about you Ms. Fletcher?

IMOGENE. Well...I don't know...I've never been on a *real* *(Beat.)* honeymoon.

BEATRICE. A what?

MAUDE. Honeymoon?

EADDY. What are you talking about?

IMOGENE. Girls...um...Sam's coming with us.

MAUDE, BEATRICE & EADDY. He is? What? Huh?

(**SAM** *enters, smiling. He takes* **IMOGENE**'s *hand.*)

IMOGENE. Last night after the chaos died down...I got a visit from Frank. He came to my room and gave me three thousand dollars and he apologized for having been an asshole...actually that is exactly what he said too..."Mom, I'm sorry I was an asshole."

BEATRICE. What did you say?

IMOGENE. What do you think I said...what do we always say to our kids when they act like asses? I said, "That's OK asshole...I love you," and then I hugged him and snatched the money.

EADDY. You're such a good momma.

IMOGENE. (*To* **RUBY SUE**.) And he said his undercover work with the FBI is going to continue?

RUBY SUE. Yes...we can always use someone like Frank as a paid informant...he is *very* convincing as a lowlife drug addict...you really should be proud.

IMOGENE. (*Unsure.*) Oh...uh...I am. Thank you?

EADDY. OK...but what does that have to do with Sam?

IMOGENE. Well...even though we have only known each other for a short time...I have grown to care about Sam very deeply...and well...ya only live once...and my time is more than half over...so...last night after Frank left... I...I asked Sam to marry me.

(**EADDY**, **BEATRICE**, *and* **IMOGENE** *gasp and react.*)

BEATRICE. Marry you...as in...till death do us part...marry you?

SAM. And I said yes.

(*Another loud gasp.*)

IMOGENE. I decided to use the money Frank gave me for our wedding and honeymoon. So I called the cruise company last night and booked the honeymoon suite.

(*Gushing.*) The ship's captain is going to marry us on the boat after we set sail...and I want *y'all* to be my bridesmaids.

> (**IMOGENE** *and* **SAM** *embrace and kiss.*)

MAUDE. Oh my God this is so romantic.

EADDY. I can't believe it.

BEATRICE. I'm nauseous –

RUBY SUE. Yes, well...I need to check with our nurses and make sure they have everything they need. Doctor Head will be back in a few days...oh...and ladies we will need depositions when you get back. Thank you again...we could not have made this case without you.

> (**RUBY SUE** *exits down left.*)

EADDY. Bye Bye.

MAUDE. Thank you.

IMOGENE. Sam honey...will you take the last of the luggage to the car?

SAM. Of course I will doll...but it's gonna cost you.

> (**IMOGENE** *kisses* **SAM** *and then he takes the last of the luggage and exits right.*)

BEATRICE. Imogene, have you just completely lost your mind? You have only known Sam for a little over a week.

MAUDE. (*Starry-eyed.*) I guess it was love at first sight.

IMOGENE. (*Romantic.*) Yes I guess it was.

BEATRICE. Well...I think it's –

EADDY. Shut up Beatty...do *not* spoil this for Imogene

BEATRICE. Fine...whatever...just as long as I don't have to wear a hideous bridesmaids dress.

IMOGENE. Actually...we are just going to wear whatever we want to...maybe we will just say our "I Do's" in our bathing suits –

> (**BEATRICE** *opens her mouth to speak but before she can,* **IMOGENE** *cuts her off.*)

And yes Beatrice...before you ask...you can wear your hot pink thong.

> (**BEATRICE** *smiles and they embrace and giggle. As they embrace,* **BEATRICE** *realizes that* **IMOGENE** *is no longer wearing her oxygen.*)

BEATRICE. Imogene...honey...where's your oxygen?

IMOGENE. You know girls...it's the weirdest thing...but with you all in my life...and now Sam...I don't need it...I feel like I am actually living for the first time in my life... and I can breathe again.

BEATRICE. I really am happy for you...old gal.

EADDY. Me too –

MAUDE. Me three.

> (*The ladies embrace in a giant ball of love as* **SAM** *enters, carrying Maude's funeral notebook.*)

SAM. Mm mm mm...I sure would like to be the ham in the middle of that sam-mitch!

IMOGENE. (*Giggling.*) Oh Sam...stop it.

EADDY. Some things will never change.

IMOGENE. (*To* **SAM**.) Let's go baby...we can sit in the back seat and make out like teenagers on the way there.

> (*She takes his hand.*)

SAM. Hubba Hubba.

> (*To* **MAUDE**.) Oh Maude...I found your funeral notebook in the garbage can out front.

> (**SAM** *tries to give the notebook to* **MAUDE** *but she waves him off.*)

MAUDE. Thank you Sam...but you can just toss it back in the trash where I put it...I've decided I want to plan my living years with my friends from now on.

> (*To* **IMOGENE**.) C'mon...I'll sit in the back with y'all...I want to live vicariously through your romance –

> (*The three exit right.*)

BEATRICE. Well...I guess I'll drive...if I don't we'll never get there...*you* drive like an old lady...let's go –

EADDY. I'll be out there in a second...go on and put on the air conditioning in the Lincoln.

(**BEATRICE** *turns to exit and then turns back.*)

BEATRICE. If you're praying...please put in a good word for me.

EADDY. Of course Mary Magdalene...

BEATRICE. *(Yelling as she exits.)* Imogene! Bring your oxygen anyway...I may want to hit it –

(**BEATRICE** *exits.* **EADDY** *puts her hands up to pray.*)

EADDY. Well Lord...it's me again and I *really* need you this time. As I'm sure you know...I am going on a cruise with four *big time* sinners...and I *know* they are going to try and drag me into their world of sin and debauchery. But here's the thing...I think I might want to...um...get involved...just a little *(She quickly looks up.)* just this once...I promise I won't get carried away. I *might* just have one of those fruity drinks with the little umbrellas...and...*maybe* if a handsome man asks me to dance...I *might* try to see what all the fuss is about. I'm not saying I am going to...you know...but maybe just a little smooching. Um anyway...I am asking you to please not strike me dead or sink the ship if I get a little too carried away just this once...OK? Oh and my friend Beatrice wanted me to put in a good word for –

(From offstage we hear **BEATRICE** *call out.)*

BEATRICE. Eaddy...where the hell are you? Get your butt in gear. Let's go...let's go!

EADDY. Never mind...screw her...she's on her own... AMEN!

(**EADDY** *jumps up and exits right as the lights fade.)*

(Curtain.)

www.ingramcontent.com/pod-product-compliance
Ingram Content Group UK Ltd.
Pitfield, Milton Keynes, MK11 3LW, UK
UKHW031553170425
457560UK00006B/228

9 780573 707162